COWBOY ABOVE THE LAW

USA TODAY Bestselling Author

DELORES FOSSEN

For devoted reader Betty Kincaid, who passed along her love of books to her children and grandchildren. Betty, you'll be missed.

Recycling programs for this product may not exist in your area.

ISBN-13: 978-1-335-63931-8

Cowboy Above the Law

This edition published by arrangement with Harlequin Books S.A.

For questions and comments about the quality of this book, please contact us at CustomerService@Harlequin.com.

Printed in U.S.A.

"I know this isn't comfortable for you..."

Rayna's voice was a hoarse whisper now. "It's okay if you put me in someone else's protective custody."

It wasn't okay. Court refused to let their past play into this. "I'll do my job," he said but hated that it came out rough and edged with too much emotion. "Or rather, I'll do my job better than I have so far. I nearly let you get killed."

"You nearly got yourself killed protecting me," she corrected. "I don't want anything happening to you because of me." She looked him in the eyes as she spoke.

That riled him. And gave him an unwanted jolt of memories. Memories of what used to be between them. Memories of Rayna.

Then her expression changed, and he saw something more than the feigned strength in her eyes.

Hell.

Rayna had almost certainly gotten a jolt of those memories, too.

Court didn't move. Neither did she. That wasn't good.

Because he was thinking about doing something like kissing her.

Delores Fossen, a *USA TODAY* bestselling author, has sold over fifty novels, with millions of copies of her books in print worldwide. She's received a Booksellers' Best Award and an RT Reviewers' Choice Best Book Award. She was also a finalist for a prestigious RITA® Award. You can contact the author through her website at www.deloresfossen.com.

Books by Delores Fossen

Harlequin Intrigue

The Lawmen of McCall Canyon

Cowboy Above the Law

Blue River Ranch

Always a Lawman
Gunfire on the Ranch
Lawman from Her Past
Roughshod Justice

The Lawmen of Silver Creek Ranch

Grayson
Dade
Nate
Kade
Gage
Mason
Josh
Sawyer
Landon
Holden

HQN Books

A Wrangler's Creek Novel

Lone Star Cowboy (ebook novella)
Those Texas Nights
One Good Cowboy (ebook novella)
No Getting Over a Cowboy
Just Like a Cowboy (ebook novella)
Branded as Trouble
Cowboy Dreaming (ebook novella)
Texas-Sized Trouble
Cowboy Heartbreaker (ebook novella)
Lone Star Blues
Cowboy Blues (ebook novella)
The Last Rodeo

Visit the Author Profile page at Harlequin.com.

CAST OF CHARACTERS

Deputy Court McCall—Court usually goes by the book when it comes to serving up justice, but he might have to bend the law to protect his old flame from a killer.

Rayna Travers—Three years ago she was accused of a crime that she didn't commit. Now, to stop someone from murdering her, she must turn to Court, but just being with him also makes him a target.

Warren McCall—When this former sheriff's secret life comes to light, it creates a dangerous situation that tears his family apart. Worse, someone's now trying to kill him.

Helen McCall—Warren's wife of forty years. She's devastated by her husband's secret and could be mentally unstable. But would she go so far as to commit a deadly crime?

Whitney Goble—Rayna's best friend, but Whitney could have her own motives for getting rid of Rayna.

Bobby Joe Hawley—The local bad boy everyone thought was dead, but did he fake his own death so that his ex, Rayna, would be convicted of his murder?

Mitch Hawley—Bobby Joe's hothead brother who might do anything to get back at Rayna since he still believes she killed Bobby Joe.

Alma Lawton—When her secret life with Warren is uncovered, she immediately becomes a suspect in the attacks on Warren and Rayna, but someone might be setting her up.

Chapter One

Deputy Court McCall glanced down at the blood on his shirt. *His father's blood.* Just the sight of it sliced away at him and made him feel as if someone had put a bullet in him, too.

Court hadn't changed into clean clothes because he wanted Rayna Travers to see what she had done. He wanted to be right in her face when he told her that she'd failed.

Barely though.

His father, Warren, was still alive, hanging on by a thread, but Court refused to accept that he wouldn't make it. No, his father would not only recover, but Warren would also help Court put Rayna behind bars. This time, she wasn't going to get away with murder.

Court pulled to a stop in front of her house, a place not exactly on the beaten path. Of course, that applied to a lot of the homes in or near McCall Canyon. His ancestors had founded the town over a hundred years ago, and it had become exactly what they'd intended it to be—a ranching community.

What they almost certainly hadn't counted on was having a would-be killer in their midst.

Court looked down at his hands. Steady. That was good. Because there was nothing steady inside him. The anger was bubbling up, and he had to make sure he reined in his temper enough to arrest Rayna. He wouldn't resort to strong-arm tactics, but there was a high chance he would say something he shouldn't.

Since Rayna's car was in her driveway, it probably meant she was home. Good. He hadn't wanted to go hunting for her. Still, it was somewhat of a surprise that she hadn't gone on the run. Of course, she was probably going to say she was innocent, that she hadn't had anything to do with the shot that'd slammed into his father's chest. But simply put, she had a strong motive to kill a McCall.

And then there was the witness.

If Rayna tried to convince him she'd had no part in the shooting, then Court would let her know that someone had spotted her in the vicinity of the sheriff's office just minutes before Warren had been gunned down. Then Court would follow through on her arrest.

He got out of his truck and started toward the porch of the small stone-front house, but Court made it only a few steps because his phone rang, and his brother's name popped up on the screen.

Egan.

Egan wasn't just his big brother though. He was also Court's boss, since Egan was the sheriff of McCall Canyon. By now, Egan had probably figured out where Court was heading and wanted to make sure his deputy followed the book on this one.

He would.

Not cutting corners because he wanted Rayna behind bars.

Court ignored the call, and the ding of the voice mail that followed, and went up the steps to the front door. This wasn't his first time here. Once, he'd made many trips to Rayna's door—before she'd chosen another man over him. Once, he'd had feelings for her. He had feelings now, too, but they had nothing to do with the old attraction he'd once felt.

He steeled himself and put his hand over his firearm in case Rayna wasn't finished with her shooting spree today.

"Open up," Court said, knocking on the door. Of course, he knocked a lot louder than necessary, but he wanted to make sure she heard him.

If she did hear him, she darn sure didn't answer. He knocked again, his anger rising even more, and Court finally tested the knob. Unlocked. So, he threw open the door.

And he found a gun pointed right in his face.

Rayna's finger was on the trigger.

Court cursed and automatically drew his own weapon. Obviously, it was too late because she could have fired before he'd even had a chance to do that. She didn't though. Maybe because Rayna felt she'd already fulfilled her quota of shooting McCalls today.

"Put down your gun," he snarled.

"No." Rayna shook her head, and that was when he noticed there was blood in her blond hair. Blood on the side of her face, too. Added to that, he could see bruises and cuts on her knuckles and wrists. "I'm not going to let you try to kill me again."

"Again?" Court was certain he looked very confused. Because he was. "What the devil are you talking about? I came here to arrest you for shooting my father."

If that news surprised her in the least, she didn't show it. She didn't lower her gun, either. Rayna stood there, glaring at him.

What the hell had happened here?

Court looked behind her to see if the person who'd given her those injuries was still around. There was no sign of anyone else, but the furniture in the living room had been tossed around. There was a broken lamp on the floor. More blood, too. All indications of a struggle.

"Start talking," Court demanded, making sure he sounded like the lawman that he was.

"I will. When Egan gets here."

Court cursed again. Egan definitely wasn't going to approve of Court storming out here to see her, but his brother also couldn't ignore the evidence that Rayna had shot their father. There was definitely something else going on though.

"My father's alive," Court told her. "You didn't manage to kill him after all."

She looked down at his shirt. At the blood. And Rayna glanced away as if the sight of it sickened her. Court took advantage of her glance and knocked the gun from her hand.

At least that was what he tried to do, but Rayna held on. She pushed him, and in the same motion, she turned to run. That was when Court tackled her. Her gun went flying, skittering all the way into the living room, and both Court and she landed hard on the floor.

Rayna groaned in pain. It wasn't a soft groan, and while holding her side, she scrambled away from him. Court was about to dive at her again, but he saw yet more blood. This time on the side that she was holding.

That stopped him.

"What's wrong with you? What happened?" Court snapped.

She looked around as if considering another run for it, but then her shoulders sagged as if she was surrendering.

Rayna sat up, putting her weight, and the back of her head, against the wall. She opened her mouth as if to start with that explanation, but she had to pause when her breath shuddered. She waved that off as if embarrassed by it and then hiked up her chin. It seemed to him as if she was trying to look strong.

She failed.

"When I came in from the barn about an hour ago, there was someone in my house," Rayna said, her voice still a little unsteady. "I didn't see who it was because he immediately clubbed me on the head and grabbed me from behind." She winced again when she rubbed her left side. "I think he cracked my ribs when he hit me with something."

Well, hell. Court certainly hadn't expected any of this. And reminded himself that maybe it was all a lie, to cover up for the fact that she'd committed a crime. But those wounds weren't lies. They were the real deal. That didn't mean that they weren't self-inflicted.

"I got away from him," she continued a moment later. "After he hit me a few more times. And I pulled my gun, which I had in a slide holster in the back of my jeans. That's when he left. I'm not sure where he went."

That didn't make sense. "If someone really broke in an hour ago, why didn't you call the sheriff's office right away?"

Rayna lifted her head a little and raised her eyebrow. For a simple gesture, it said loads. She didn't trust the cops. Didn't trust *him*.

Well, the feeling was mutual.

"I passed out for a while," she added. She shook her head as if even she was confused by that, and she lifted the side of her shirt that had the blood. There was a bruise there, too, and what appeared to be a puncture wound. One that had likely caused the bleeding. "Or maybe the guy drugged me."

"Great," he muttered. This was getting more

far-fetched with each passing moment. "FYI, I'm not buying this. And as for not calling the cops when you were attacked, you called Egan when you saw me," Court pointed out.

"Because I didn't want things to escalate to this." She motioned to their positions on the floor. "Obviously, it didn't work."

He huffed. "And neither is this story you're telling." Court got to his feet and took out his phone. "Only a couple of minutes before my father was gunned down, a waitress in the diner across the street from the sheriff's office spotted you in the parking lot. There's no way you could have been here in your house during this so-called attack because you were in town."

She quit wincing so she could glare at him. "I was here." Her tone said *I don't care if you believe me or not.*

He didn't believe her. "You must have known my father had been shot because you didn't react when I told you."

"I did know. Whitney called me when I was walking back from the barn. I'd just gotten off the phone with her when that goon clubbed me."

Whitney Goble, her best friend. And it was entirely possible that Whitney had either seen his father get shot or heard about it shortly thereafter because she worked part-time as a dispatcher for the sheriff's office. It would be easy enough to check to see if Whitney had indeed called her, and using her cell phone records, they could possibly figure out Rayna's location when she'd talked to her friend. Court was betting it hadn't been on Rayna's walk back from the barn. It had been while she was escaping from the scene of the shooting.

"This waitress claims she saw me shoot your father?" Rayna asked.

He hated that he couldn't answer yes to that, but Court couldn't. "She was in the kitchen when the actual shot was fired. But the bullet came from the park directly behind the sheriff's office parking lot. The very parking lot where you were right before the attack."

Judging from her repeated flat look, Rayna was about to deny that, so Court took out his phone and opened the photo. "The waitress took that picture of you."

Court didn't go closer to her with the phone, but Rayna stood. Not easily. She continued to clutch her side and blew out some short, rough breaths. However, she shook her head the moment her attention landed on the grainy shot of the woman in a red dress. A woman with hair the same color blond as Rayna's.

"That's not me," she insisted. "I don't have a dress that color. And besides, I wasn't there."

This was a very frustrating conversation, but thankfully he had more. He tapped the car that was just up the street from the woman in the photo. "That's your car, your license plate."

With her forehead bunched up, Rayna snatched the phone from him and had a closer look. "That's not my car. I've been home all morning." Her gaze flew to his, and now there was some venom in her eyes. "You're trying to set me up." She groaned and practically threw his phone at him. "Haven't you McCalls already done enough to me without adding this?"

Court caught his phone, but he had to answer her through clenched teeth. "We haven't done anything."

She laughed, but there wasn't a trace of humor in it. "Right. Remember Bobby Joe?" she spat out. "Or did you forget about him?"

Bobby Joe Hawley. No, Court hadn't forgotten. Obviously, neither had Rayna.

"Three years ago, your father tried to pin Bobby Joe's murder on me," Rayna continued. "It didn't work. A jury acquitted me."

He couldn't deny the acquittal. "Being found not guilty isn't the same as being innocent."

Something that ate away at him. Because the evidence had been there. Bobby Joe's blood in Rayna's house. Blood that she'd tried to clean up. There'd also been the knife found in her barn. It'd had Bobby Joe's blood on it, too. What was missing were Rayna's prints. Ditto for the body. They'd never found it, but Rayna could have hidden it along with wiping her prints from the murder weapon.

The jury hadn't seen it that way though.

Possibly because they hadn't been able to look past one other piece of evidence. Bobby Joe had assaulted Rayna on several occasions, both while they'd been together and after their breakup when she'd gotten a restraining order against him. In her mind, she probably thought that was justification to kill him. And equal justification to now go after Court's father, who'd been sheriff at the time. Warren had been the one to press for Rayna's arrest and trial. After that, his father had retired. But Rayna could have been holding a serious grudge against him all this time.

She'd certainly held one against Court.

He heard the sound of a vehicle pulling up in front of Rayna's house and knew it was Egan before he glanced out the still-open door. He also knew Egan wouldn't be pleased. And he was right. His brother was sporting a scowl when he got out of the cruiser and started for the door.

Egan was only two years older than Court, but he definitely had that "big brother, I'm in charge" air about him. Egan had somehow managed to have that even when he'd still been a deputy. Folks liked to joke that he could kick your butt even before you'd known it was kicked.

"If you think Egan is going to let you walk, think again," Court warned her.

"I won't let him railroad me," she insisted, aiming another scowl at Court. "I won't let you do it, either. It doesn't matter that we have a history together. That history gives you no right to pull some stunt like this."

They had a history all right. Filled with both good and bad memories. They'd been high school sweethearts, but that "young love" was significantly overshadowed by the bad blood that was between them now.

Egan stepped into the house, putting his hands on his hips, and made a sweeping glance around the room before his attention landed on

Court. "Please tell me you're not responsible for any of this."

"I'm not." At least Court hoped he wasn't, but it was possible he'd added some to the damage when he tackled her. "Rayna said someone broke in."

Court figured his brother was also going to have a hard time believing that. It did seem too much of a coincidence that his father would be shot and Rayna would have a break-in around the same time.

"You shouldn't have come," Egan said to him in a rough whisper.

Court was certain he'd hear more of that later, but he had a darn good reason for being here. "I didn't want her to escape."

"And I thought he'd come here to kill me," Rayna countered. "I pulled a gun on him." She swallowed hard. "Things didn't go well after that."

Egan huffed and grumbled something that Court didn't catch before he took out his phone and texted someone.

"Court didn't do any of the damage in this room," Rayna added. "It happened when an intruder attacked me."

That only tightened Egan's mouth even more before he shifted his gaze to Rayna. "An ambulance is on the way. How bad are you hurt?" he asked and put his phone back in his pocket.

She waved it off, wincing again while she did that. Yeah, she was hurt. But Court thought Egan was missing what was really important here.

"She shot Dad," Court reminded Egan. "We have the picture, remember?" Though he knew there was no way his brother could have forgotten that. "It's proof she was there. Proof that she shot him."

"No, it's not." Egan groaned, scrubbed his hand over his face. "I think someone tried to set Rayna up."

Court opened his mouth to say that wasn't true. But then Egan took out his own phone and showed him a picture.

"A few minutes after you stormed out of the hospital," Egan continued, "Eldon Cooper, the clerk at the hardware store, found this."

"This" was a blond-haired woman wearing a red dress. An identical dress to the one in the photo the waitress had taken. But this one had one big difference from the first picture.

In this one, the woman was dead.

Chapter Two

Rayna slowly walked toward Egan so she could see the photograph that had caused Court to go stiff. It had caused him to mumble some profanity, too, and Rayna soon knew why.

The woman in the photograph had been shot in the head.

There was blood. Her body was limp, and her lifeless eyes were fixed in a permanent blank stare at the sky.

Rayna dropped back a step, an icy chill going through her. Because Court had been right. The woman did look like her. The one in the first picture did, anyway. The second photo was much clearer, and while it wasn't a perfect match, the dead woman looked enough like her to be a relative. But Rayna knew she didn't have any living relatives.

"Someone killed her because of me?" she whispered.

Neither Court nor Egan denied it.

She felt the tears threaten. The panic, too. But Rayna forced herself not to give in to either of them. Not in front of Court, anyway. Later, she could have a cry, tend to her wounds and try to figure out what the heck was going on.

"Who is she?" Rayna asked.

"We don't have an ID on her yet, but we will soon. After the medical examiner's had a look at her, then we'll search for any ID. If there isn't any on her body or in the car, we'll run her prints."

It was so hard for Rayna to think with her head hurting, but she forced herself to try to figure this out. "Why would someone go to all the trouble of having a look-alike and then leave a car behind with bogus plates?"

Egan shrugged again. "It goes back to someone setting you up." He sounded a little skeptical about that though. "Unless you hired the woman in that photo to pose as you. You could have gotten spooked when something went wrong and left the car."

Even though she'd braced herself to have more accusations tossed at her, that still stung. It always did. Because this accusation went beyond just hiring an impostor. He was almost certainly implying that she had something to do with the woman's death, too.

"No. I didn't hire her," Rayna managed to say, though her throat had clamped shut. "And I didn't shoot your father. I haven't been in town in weeks, and that wasn't my car parked near the sheriff's office."

Egan nodded, glanced at Court. "She's right about the car. The plates are fake. I had one of the deputies go out and take a look at it. It's still parked up the street from the office. Someone painted over the numbers so that it matched the plates on Rayna's vehicle."

Again, Egan was making it sound as if she had something to do with that. Good grief. Why was she always having to defend herself when it came to the McCalls?

Of course, she knew the answer.

She'd made her own bed when it'd come to Bobby Joe. She had stayed with him even after he'd hit her and called her every name in the book. She had let him rob her of her confidence. Her dignity.

And nearly her life.

But Egan and Court—and their father—hadn't seen things that way. Bobby Joe had kept the abuse hidden. A wolf in sheep's clothing, and very few people in town had been on her side when Warren McCall had arrested her for Bobby Joe's murder.

"You're barking up the wrong tree—again," Rayna added. "I didn't have anything to do with this. And why would I? If I were going to shoot anyone, why would I send in a look-alike? Why would I pick a spot like Main Street, which is practically on the doorstep of a building filled with cowboy cops?"

Egan shrugged. "Maybe to make us believe you're innocent and knew nothing about it."

"I am innocent," she practically yelled. Rayna stopped though and peered at the mess in the living room. "But maybe my intruder is behind what happened in town and what happened to that woman, as well. He could have arranged to have your father shot, killed her, and then he could have come out here to attack me. His prints could be on the lamp. It's what he used to bash me over the head."

Court looked at her, and for a split second, she thought she saw some sympathy in his intense gray eyes. It was gone as quickly as it'd come, and he stood there, waiting. Maybe for an explanation that would cause all of this to make sense. But she couldn't give him that.

Rayna huffed. "If I was going to do something to fake an assault, I wouldn't have hit myself that hard on my head or cracked my ribs. And I wouldn't have broken my grandmother's lamp."

It sickened her to see it shattered like that. In the grand scheme of things, it wasn't a huge deal, but it felt like one to her. It was one of the few things she had left of her gran. And now it was gone—much like what little peace of mind she'd managed to regain over the past year.

"Who do you think would have done something like this?" Court asked, tipping his head toward the living room.

"Bobby Joe," she answered without thinking. She knew it would get huffs and eye rolls from them, and it did. "You think he's dead, that I killed him. But I know I didn't. So, that means he could still be out there."

Court didn't repeat his huff, but she could tell he wanted to. "So, you think Bobby Joe set you up for my father's shooting and then came out here and attacked you? If he's really alive, why would he wait three years to do that?"

Rayna gave it some thought and didn't have an answer. However, she wouldn't put it past Bobby Joe. At the end of their relationship, he'd threatened to kill her. Maybe this was his way of doing that. Bobby Joe could be toying with her while also getting back at Warren

McCall, who hadn't managed to get her convicted of murder.

But there was something else. A piece that didn't seem to fit.

"Tell me about the waitress," Rayna insisted. "Who was she, and why did she take the picture of the woman in the parking lot?"

"Her name is Janet Bolin," Court answered. "She said she took the photo because she thought you…or rather the woman…was acting strange."

Egan groaned. Probably because he was agreeing with her theory of an ill-fitting puzzle piece. "I'll get a CSI team out here to process the place." He pressed a button on his phone and went onto the porch to make the call.

"You know this waitress?" Rayna asked Court.

He shook his head. "She's new, has only been working there a week or so, but I've seen her around. We'll bring her in for questioning."

Good. Because it meant Rayna was finally making some headway in convincing Court that she hadn't fired that shot or had anything to do with that woman's death.

She hesitated before asking her next question. "How's your father?" Warren was a touchy subject for both of them.

A muscle flickered in Court's jaw. "He's out of surgery but still unconscious. We don't know just how bad the damage is yet."

He might have added more, might, but a sound outside stopped him. Sirens. They were from the ambulance that was coming up the road. Since her house was the only one out here, they were here for her.

"I don't want an ambulance," she insisted. "I'll go to the hospital on my own." And it wouldn't be to the one in McCall Canyon. She would drive into nearby San Antonio.

"That's not a very smart thing to do." No pause for Court that time. "We're not sure what's going on here. Plus, your ribs could be broken. You don't need to be driving if they are."

She couldn't help it. Rayna gave him a snarky smile before she could stop herself. "Worried about me?"

That earned her another glare, but this one didn't last. And for a moment she saw something else. Not the sympathy this time, either. But the old attraction. Even now, it tugged at her. Apparently, it tugged at Court because he cursed again and looked away.

"I just wanted to make sure I didn't hurt you when we fell on the floor," Court said.

"You didn't." That was probably a lie, but Rayna was hurting in so many places that it was hard to tell who was responsible for the bruises and cuts.

Court's gaze came back to her. "Was there anything...sexual about the assault after you got hit on the head?"

"No." Thank God. That was something at least. "In fact, I'm not even sure he intended to kill me. I mean, he could have shot me the moment I walked into my house—"

"Maybe he didn't have a gun. He could have been robbing the place and got spooked when you came in."

True. But that didn't feel right. Neither did the spot on her ribs, and Rayna had another look. Too bad that meant pulling up her top again, and this time Court examined it, too. He leaned in, so close that she could feel his breath hitting her skin.

"It looks like a needle mark," he said. "And you mentioned something about passing out?"

She nodded. "But the man was gone by the time that happened." Of course, he could have come back. Heck, he could still come back.

That made her stomach tighten, and she gave an uneasy glance around the front and side yards. There were plenty of places on her land for someone to hide.

"You're sure it was a man?" Court asked. He was using his lawman's tone again. Good. That was easier to deal with than the old attraction. "You said you didn't get a look at the person, so how do you know it was a man?"

"I've had a man's hands on me before, so yes, I'm sure he was male." She immediately hated that she'd blurted that out, even if it was true. But Rayna didn't like reminding anyone, especially Court, of just how wrong she'd been about Bobby Joe. After all, she'd let Court go to be with him.

"After he clubbed me with the lamp," Rayna added, "he hooked his arm around my throat. My back landed against his chest, so I know it was a man."

Court took a moment, obviously processing that, and he looked at the lock on the front door. "There's no sign of forced entry. Was it locked, and did you have on your security system?"

Everything inside her went still. With all the chaos that had gone on, it hadn't occurred to Rayna to ask herself those questions. "Yes, it would have been locked, and the security system was on. I never leave the house without doing that."

"Even if you were just going to the barn?" Court immediately asked.

"Even then." She gathered her breath, which had suddenly gone thin again. It always did when she thought of the woman she'd become. "I honestly believe Bobby Joe is alive and that he could come after me."

Court looked ready to grumble out some profanity, but Rayna wasn't sure if that was because he felt sorry for her or because he thought she was crazy for being so wary about a man he believed was dead.

"The front door was unlocked when I got here," Court continued several moments later. "Is it possible your intruder had a key?"

"No. And I don't keep a spare one lying around, either." She kept her attention on the ambulance that stopped behind the cruiser. "Plus, he would have had to disarm the security system. It's tamperproof, so he couldn't have simply cut a wire or something. He would have had to know the code."

With each word, that knot in her stomach got tighter and tighter. She had taken all the necessary precautions, and it hadn't been enough. That hurt. Because she might never feel safe here again in this house that she loved. Her gran's house. That didn't mean she would leave. No. She wouldn't give Bobby Joe the satisfaction of seeing her run, but Rayna figured there'd be a lot more sleepless nights in her future.

Egan was still on the phone when the medics got out of the ambulance and started for the porch. Rayna went out to tell them they could leave, but she spotted another vehicle. A familiar one.

Whitney's red Mustang.

"You called her?" Court asked.

Rayna shook her head, but it didn't surprise her that Whitney had heard about what happened and then had driven out to see her. They'd been friends since third grade, and even though that friendship had cooled a little after Rayna had gotten involved with Bobby Joe, Whitney had usually been there for her. Whitney was also one of the few people who'd stood by her when Rayna had been on trial.

Her friend bolted from the car and ran past the medics to get to Rayna. Whitney immediately pulled her into her arms for a hug. An uncomfortable one because Rayna felt the pain from her ribs, and she backed away.

"I came as fast as I could get someone to

cover for me at work." Whitney's words rushed together. "My God, you're hurt." She reached out as if to touch the wound on Rayna's hand, but she stopped. "It must be bad if the ambulance came."

"No. They were just leaving." Rayna made sure she said that loud enough for the medics to hear.

"They're not leaving," Court snapped, and he motioned for them to wait. No doubt so he could try to talk Rayna into going with them.

Whitney volleyed puzzled looks between Court and her. "Is, uh, anything going on between you two? I mean, you're not back together, are you?"

"No," Court and Rayna answered in unison, but it did make Rayna wonder what Whitney had picked up on to make her think that.

Whitney released her breath as if relieved. Maybe because she knew Rayna wasn't ready for a relationship. Especially one with Court McCall.

"What happened here?" Whitney asked, glancing inside.

"Someone broke in," Rayna settled for saying. She planned to give Whitney more information later, but her friend filled in the blanks.

"And you think it was Bobby Joe," Whitney concluded. But she immediately shook her head after saying that. "It seems to be more than that going on. I mean, what with Warren being shot."

Court made a sound of agreement. "Do you have a key to Rayna's house? And no, I'm not accusing her of anything," Court quickly added to Rayna. "I'm just trying to figure out how the intruder got in."

"No key," Whitney answered. "Bobby Joe wouldn't have one, either. Rayna changed all the locks after she was acquitted. She had the windows and doors wired for security, too. Did she tell you that she has guns stashed all around the house?"

Rayna gave Whitney a sharp look to get her to hush. But it was too late. After hearing that, Court was probably even more convinced that she was about to go off the deep end.

"So, are you coming with us?" one of the medics called out. He sounded, and looked, impatient.

Rayna knew him. His name was Dustin Mendoza. A friend of Bobby Joe's. Of course, pretty much every man in McCall Canyon in their midthirties fell into that particular category.

"No," Rayna repeated.

She figured Court was about to do some repeating as well and insist that she go. He didn't. "I'll drive Rayna to the hospital. I need to ask her some more questions about the break-in."

Dustin didn't wait around to see if that was okay with her. He motioned for his partner to leave, and they started back for the ambulance.

"I also think you should consider protective custody," Court said to her. "The intruder obviously knows how to get in your house, and he could come back."

That had already occurred to Rayna, but it chilled her to the bone to hear someone say it.

"You can stay with me," Whitney suggested. "In fact, I can take you to the hospital."

It was generous of Whitney, and Rayna was about to consider accepting, but Court spoke before she could say anything. "That could be dangerous. For Whitney. If this intruder is still after you, he could go to her place while looking for you."

That drained some of the color from Whitney's face. Obviously, it wasn't something she'd considered when she'd made the offer.

"It's okay," Rayna assured her. "I can make other plans."

She didn't know what exactly those plans would be, but she might have to hire a bodyguard. And put some distance between her and the McCalls. Whatever was going on seemed to be connected to them. Rayna didn't think it was a coincidence about the timing of Warren's attack, the break-in and the dead woman.

Egan finally finished his call, and the moment he turned to walk toward them, Rayna knew something was wrong.

"Is it Dad?" Court immediately asked.

Egan shook his head. "It's the waitress. Janet Bolin. She's dead. Someone murdered her."

Chapter Three

Another murder. Two women killed only hours apart. There was no way Court could dismiss them as not being connected.

But connected to what?

Rayna. His father. Or maybe both.

He put on a clean shirt that he took from his locker and thought about that possible connection while he made his way back into the squad room, where Rayna was waiting. Or rather where she was pacing. He nearly reminded her that she should probably be sitting down. That was what the doctor had wanted anyway when he'd come to the sheriff's office to examine her. Rayna wasn't having any part of that though. And he couldn't blame her. It was hard to sit still with all this restless energy bubbling up inside him.

"Anything?" she asked the moment she saw him.

Court took a deep breath that sounded as weary as he felt. "There's no gunshot residue on your hands." He'd swabbed her hands as soon as they'd gotten to the sheriff's office but hadn't been able to run the test right away because of all the other calls.

And changing his shirt.

Court had figured he'd worn his father's blood long enough and no longer wanted it in his sight.

Rayna didn't huff, but it was close. "Tell me something I don't know. Of course there wasn't gunshot residue on my hands, because I didn't fire a gun."

He almost pointed out that she could have cleaned up afterward, but plain and simple, that probably hadn't happened. And it wouldn't explain how she'd gotten all those wounds. So, Court did as Rayna asked and gave her something she almost certainly didn't know.

"Janet was killed with a single shot to the head at point-blank range. Her body was in the alley behind the diner, and it doesn't appear as if she was moved after she was shot. No ID yet on the other woman."

But the two had something in common. There'd been no defensive wounds, which meant their killer had gotten close enough to deliver the fatal shots without alarming the women.

"No one in or around the diner heard the shot?" she pressed.

"No. But she had her purse, and Pete, the cook, said she had three more hours on her shift. She didn't have a cell phone on her, but maybe she'd made arrangements to meet someone."

And that *someone* had killed her.

That could mean Janet was in on his father's shooting. Or maybe she'd just been duped into taking the photo that had almost certainly been meant to frame Rayna.

"There aren't any surveillance cameras back there," Court added. That pretty much applied to most of the town. Simply put, there hadn't been much need for them.

Until now, that was.

There'd been only two murders in the past ten years. A drunken brawl at the local bar and Bobby Joe's. But now they had two unsolved homicides, an attempted murder, breaking and entering, and an assault. It was no wonder Egan had been tied up in the past three hours. His brother was at the first murder scene, and that was why Court had been manning the phones along with keeping an eye on Rayna.

Court hadn't mentioned it yet, but she was now a key witness, since she might be able to recall something about the man who'd attacked her. She was almost certainly in grave danger, as well.

"It doesn't make sense," Rayna mumbled.

It was something she'd said multiple times after Court had insisted that she come to the sheriff's office. Well, first he'd tried to talk her into going to the hospital, and when he'd failed at that, he'd brought her here instead. It was far better than her being at Whitney's, and both Rayna and she had finally agreed on that. Rayna had also agreed on the doctor seeing her.

"How are your ribs and your head?" Court asked.

"Fine," she answered, practically waving off his concern.

But he knew there had to be some pain. The doctor didn't think her ribs were broken, but there was a deep bruise, and a second one on her head where the intruder had hit her.

"The doctor drew blood," she added, rubbing the inside of her arm. "Whatever the thug slammed into me might still be in my system."

Yeah, but it might not give them any new info to catch him. Still, it was something they needed to know so they could make sure it didn't have any serious side effects.

He tipped his head toward Egan's office, which was just off the squad room. "There's a semicomfortable chair in there. Some bottled water, too. You could sit and wait while I call the lab and push them to get an ID on the first woman."

Rayna stopped pacing and made eye contact with him. "You're being nice to me."

Was he? Court lifted his shoulder. "I just figured we could call a truce and try to get through this hellish day."

Rayna kept staring at him a moment before she nodded and headed for the office. Court was right behind her, but he glanced around the squad room first to make sure all was well. There was only one other deputy, Thea Morris, who was taking a statement from another waitress who worked at the diner. The other four deputies were out at their three crime scenes.

"If you want to go to the hospital to see your dad," Rayna said, "please do. I know you'd rather be with him."

He would. But his father was still unconscious, so there was nothing Court could do. Plus, his mom, Helen, and his sister, Rachel, were there. Along with a Texas Ranger, Griff

Morris, who Warren had practically raised. He was like family, and he'd call Court if there were any changes in his father's condition. Or if any more trouble surfaced. Right now, Court would do his dad more good by trying to figure out who'd put that bullet in him.

"You don't have to babysit me," Rayna added.

He did indeed have to do just that, and Court didn't bother to pull any punches when he looked at her.

"Oh," she said, and Rayna looked even more unsteady when she sank into the chair across from the desk.

"It's not personal," he added because he thought that might help. Help who exactly, Court didn't know. It certainly felt personal. And it couldn't. He couldn't let their past—either the good or the bad parts—play into this.

He made the call to the lab, promptly got put on hold, so while he was waiting, Court took a copy of her statement that he'd printed out and passed it to her.

"Look this over and try to fill in any gaps in details," he instructed. "For instance, do you remember hearing the sound of a vehicle when your attacker fled?"

"No." Rayna sounded steady enough when

she said that, but when Court gave her a closer look, he saw that she was blinking back tears. Waving them off, too, when she realized he'd noticed.

"I hate this," she said. "I've spent three years rebuilding my life, and now it feels as if it's falling apart again."

Court had no idea how to respond to that, so he stayed quiet, fished out a box of tissues from the bottom drawer and passed them to her.

"I took self-defense classes," she went on. "Firearms training. I installed a security system and don't go anywhere without a gun. Except here, of course."

He would have liked to have told her there was no need for one here, that she was under the roof with two deputies, but since his father had been shot just yards from here, he doubted his words would give her much assurance. Plus, there was the part about her not trusting him.

"You did all of that because you were afraid of Bobby Joe returning?" Court tried to keep his tone neutral. They already had enough battles to fight without his adding some disbelief to that.

"Not afraid," Rayna said in a whisper. "I

wanted to be able to stop him if he came after me again. I learned the hard way that I can't rely on others to help me with that."

Court couldn't help himself. It was a knee-jerk reaction, but he went on the offensive, something he usually did with Rayna. "I arrested Bobby Joe after you'd had enough of him and decided to press charges," he reminded her.

"Yes, and he spent less than an hour in jail. After that, he threatened to kill me, stormed out and then faked his death to set me up."

If that had truly happened, then Court felt bad that he hadn't been able to do more. But that was a big *if.* Most folks had liked Bobby Joe and gotten along with him just fine.

Court wasn't one of those folks.

Bobby Joe and he had always seemed to be bristling at each other. Maybe because Rayna and Court had dated through most of high school. Bobby Joe could have been jealous, and Court figured his own bristling stemmed from the fact that Rayna had crushed his heart when she'd broken up with him.

But that was water under a very old bridge.

"Are you ever going to at least consider that Bobby Joe could be alive?" Rayna asked.

He didn't have to figure out what his answer

would be because Clyde Selby, the lab guy, finally came back on the line. "Sorry to keep you waiting," Clyde said. "I wanted to see what we had on the second woman before I spoke to you. Anyway, the first woman, the blonde, is Hallie Ramon. She is, *was*, a college student. She was in the system because of a drug arrest when she was eighteen. But she didn't have any gunshot residue on her hands, so I don't think she's the one who shot your dad."

Court felt the slam of disappointment. Whoever had done this was still out there.

He immediately pulled up everything he had on her. There wasn't much. No record other than the drug possession. The woman was twenty-four and didn't even have a traffic ticket. But then something caught his eye.

"She was a drama student." Court hadn't meant to say that aloud, but it certainly caught Rayna's attention.

She moved to the edge of her seat. Court hated to disappoint her, but there likely wouldn't be anything else from the lab. Any new info now would come from working the case, and that meant talking to Hallie's friends to find out how she was connected to what had happened in McCall Canyon.

"You mentioned the second woman," Court prompted Clyde.

"Yes. Janet Bolin. Egan sent me her prints, and there's no match for her. Don't know who she is because unlike the first woman, she's not in the system. No driver's license, nothing."

Court groaned. That meant she'd lied when she'd applied for the waitress job. Had probably even used a fake ID. That was going to make it a whole lot harder. Because until they knew who she was, they wouldn't be able to figure out how she was connected to this.

"Is she here?" someone yelled. "I want to see her now!"

Court instantly recognized the voice and knew this would be trouble. It was Mitch Hawley, Bobby Joe's brother. And the *she* that he was yelling about was almost certainly Rayna.

She got right up out of the chair and whirled to face Mitch. And not just face him. She went straight out into the squad room. If she was the least bit afraid of him, she didn't show it.

But she should have.

Unlike Bobby Joe, Mitch was not well liked, and he had a nasty temper. Court had had to arrest him on several occasions for fighting. That was why Court hurried to get between them. He didn't mind arresting Mitch again, but he didn't want the man hitting Rayna. Mitch was a big guy, around six-two, and he was heavily muscled. A build that suited him because he worked with rodeo bulls, but his fists could do a lot of damage.

"Why isn't she locked up?" Mitch snarled.

"Because I haven't done anything wrong," Rayna answered.

"Right. You killed my brother, and now you shot his dad." His gaze flew to Court. "Please tell me you're not covering for her."

"No need. There's no GSR on her, and at the time of the shooting, someone was attacking her. What do you know about that?"

That put some fire in Mitch's already fiery brown eyes. "Are you accusing me of something?"

"Not at the moment. Right now, I'm asking a question. Depending on how you answer it, I'll make an accusation or not."

Rayna shook her head, maybe asking Court not to fight her battles, but he wasn't. With everything else going on, he hadn't had time to work on who'd attacked Rayna, but because of their history, Mitch was an automatic suspect.

"No. I didn't go after her. Didn't have anything to do with this hell-storm that hit town today." Mitch snapped toward Rayna as if ready to return some verbal fire, but he stopped, smiled. "Looks like somebody worked you over good."

"Was it you who did it?" Court pressed, getting Mitch's attention back on him.

The man had to get his teeth unclenched before he could speak. "No. I wouldn't waste my time on a killer. But I can't believe you'd just let her walk. She had motive to shoot your father."

"Yeah, and so do you," Court reminded him. "In fact, I seem to remember you pressing my dad and the rest of us to put Rayna behind bars. We did, and she was acquitted. End of story."

"No, hell, no. It's not the end." He flung his index finger in her direction. "If she's capable of killing my brother, she's capable of anything."

"Apparently not," Rayna spoke up. "I'm not capable of convincing anyone that *not guilty* means I didn't do it." She spared Court a glance to let him know he fell into that category, too.

"Because you bought off the jury or something. I begged Warren to try to reopen the case against you—"

"There's no case to reopen," Court interrupted. He was getting a glimpse of what Rayna had been dealing with for the past three years. "She can't be tried again because that's double jeopardy."

"Then find something else. Conspiracy or tampering with evidence." Mitch paused only long enough to curse. "Next week is the third anniversary of my brother's murder, and no one has paid for that."

And no one might pay. Court kept that to himself though. Simply put, Rayna had been their one and only suspect.

"Why'd you go to my father with all of this?" Court asked.

Mitch huffed, clearly annoyed with that question. "I went to him because I don't get anywhere with Egan and you, that's why. I figured I could get him to sway you into doing something. Warren told me to let it go. To get a life. Can you believe that?"

Yeah, he could. Warren could be steel-hard and cold. Even though his father hated that Rayna had been acquitted, he hated even more that Mitch was blaming the McCalls for that.

Mitch rubbed his head. "I can't let it go. I keep dreaming about Bobby Joe. Nightmares. It's as if he's trying to tell me from the grave to get justice for him." He looked up, blinked, the expression of a man who felt he'd maybe said too much. Or maybe Mitch just hadn't wanted them to hear the raw emotion that was still in his voice.

"There is no new evidence to charge Rayna with anything," Court said. "Not Bobby Joe's murder and not my father's shooting."

"Then you're not looking hard enough," Mitch snarled. His face hardened. "And she's responsible for that. She's got you convinced that she's the same girl you loved back in high school. Well, she's not."

Mitch moved his hand toward Rayna as if he might take hold of her, but Court snagged his wrist.

"It's time for you to go," he warned him.

Mitch threw off Court's grip with far more force than necessary. "You should have known she'd pull something like shooting your dad. The signs were there. Even Janet said so."

Court pulled back his shoulders. "Janet?"

"Yeah, the new waitress at the diner across the street. I was in there earlier this week..." Mitch stopped. He must have realized Rayna's and Court's expressions had changed.

"What did *Janet* say about me?" Rayna demanded.

Some of that fire started to cool a bit, and

Mitch got quiet for several long moments. "She knew a lot about you. About what'd happened with Bobby Joe. She asked me questions about it."

Court jumped right on that. "What kind of questions?"

Mitch volleyed some glances at both of them and shook his head. "Things like how often Rayna came into town and such."

Bingo. It meant she was spying on Rayna. "Did Janet ever say anything about hurting Rayna or getting back at her for some reason?" Court asked.

Mitch's eyes widened. "No. Of course not. She wouldn't have. I mean, what with her being a private detective and all."

Now Court was certain his own eyes widened. "What made you think she was a PI?"

"She let it slip, and I saw her ID once when it fell out of her pocket. I thought you knew."

Court glanced at Rayna to see if she had any idea about this. She didn't. She shook her head.

"I thought you knew," Mitch repeated. "After all, Janet was working for your father. Warren's the one who hired her."

Chapter Four

Answers. That was what Rayna needed right now. Along with another place to stay. She only hoped she managed to get both soon.

Her place wasn't exactly safe, so that was why Court had brought her to the guesthouse on the grounds of his family's ranch. She felt as if she'd slept in the enemy's camp. With her enemy, since Court had stayed the night with her. She was betting though that there hadn't been much sleeping going on. There certainly hadn't been on her part. She hadn't been able to turn off her mind. Hadn't been able to forget that someone was trying to frame her for murder.

Again.

If Bobby Joe was truly behind this, then she prayed he'd just go ahead and show his face so she could put an end to this once and for all.

Since the cabin wasn't that large, Rayna had

no trouble hearing someone moving around in the kitchen. Court, no doubt, because she also smelled coffee. While she wasn't especially anxious to face him, she did need some caffeine, and maybe he would have updates that would give her those answers. Specifically, updates on his father. She needed to know if Mitch had been right when he said that Warren had hired the now dead waitress.

If he had, then maybe this was Warren's twisted way of trying to send her to jail. This time for good.

But Rayna had to mentally shake her head at that thought. From all accounts, Warren could have been killed when he was shot. If this was a plan he'd orchestrated, he wouldn't have put his life at risk like that.

Rayna took a deep breath to steady herself and walked into the kitchen. Not a long trek at all, only a few yards. She immediately saw that she'd been right about it being Court in the kitchen. Right about the coffee, too, because he was pouring himself a cup.

"You're up and dressed," he commented, sounding relieved.

That relief was probably about the being dressed part though. It would have been too much of a trip down memory lane if she'd just been wearing her nightgown—or nothing at all—since Court had brought her here a couple of times when they'd still been dating.

"I wore my clothes to bed," she said, making a beeline for the coffee. That way, if they were attacked, she would be ready to run or fight back. "I'll need to go back to my place and check on the horses."

"I sent a couple of the ranch hands over to do that. I didn't think it was a good idea for you to be out in the open like that."

No. It wasn't a smart idea, but Rayna still wished she could at least see the horses. Just being around them usually calmed her, and she desperately needed that right now.

"Thanks," she muttered. She was surprised and glad that Court had thought to do something like that. Of course, she'd probably been on his mind most of the morning, not in a good way, either.

"In case you're still in pain." Court slid a bottle of pain meds across the counter toward her. It was the prescription stuff the doctor had called into the pharmacy for her. Apparently, someone had picked it up and brought it to the ranch.

She thanked him again but wouldn't take any. Her head was already cloudy enough without adding those to the mix. "Please tell me you have good news."

His shrug didn't give her much hope. "My dad's still not conscious, so we haven't been able to ask him about Janet or whoever the heck she is. But we did get back your results from the blood test the doctor took, and you were drugged. It was a barbiturate, definitely meant to knock you out."

Then it was mission accomplished for her attacker, and he'd likely done that so she wouldn't show up in town at the same time as Hallie Ramon, the woman in red who had been near the sheriff's office. And either the woman had been there to shoot Warren or else Hallie had been set up, just as someone had attempted to do to her.

"What about you?" he asked. "You remember anything new about the person who drugged you?"

She had a long sip of coffee and shook her head. "But last night I called the company that installed my security system. They insist no one who works for them would have given out my code to disarm the system."

"Even if they had, there's the problem with the key," Court pointed out. "There were no signs of forced entry."

"No, but getting the key would have been easier than getting the security code. I don't take my house key off the ring when I give it to the mechanic for an oil change." Though she would do that in the future. "I also don't know if the locksmith I used made a copy of the key and gave it to someone."

She knew she was sounding a little paranoid, but Rayna needed to look at all angles here. Unfortunately, there were probably other times when maybe her purse, and therefore her keys, had been out of her sight long enough for someone to make a molding of the house key.

Yes, definitely paranoid.

He paused to have some coffee, as well. "Unless you forgot to lock the door. Maybe forgot to set the system, too."

Rayna was shaking her head before he finished talking. "I don't forget those things. Not after what happened with Bobby Joe. I know you don't believe it, but he's out there."

No, Court didn't believe it. She could see the doubt in his eyes. And maybe he was right.

Rayna huffed. "If Bobby Joe's dead, I didn't kill him, and that means if he's not out there, then his killer is. That's why I lock the doors. That's why I have a security system."

He made a sound that could have meant anything. "Why did you stay if you think Bobby Joe or his killer will come back?"

She heard more of those doubts, and while Rayna didn't think she could make him understand, she tried anyway. "I wasn't born into money. And, no, that's not a dig about you and your family. It's my clumsy way of saying that I can't just pick up and leave even if that's what I wanted to do."

Which she didn't. That house was her home where she'd been raised. Where once she'd been happy. She was hoping to reach that happy status again.

"Besides," Rayna added a moment later, "training horses is something I love doing, and I'm fortunate enough that it pays the bills." That along with the money she got from boarding horses from some folks who lived in town. The occasional riding lessons, too.

Court stared at her, and he obviously had something on his mind. "You never collected Bobby Joe's life insurance money. It was for fifty grand, and he left it all to you."

Yes, he had. Considering the big blowup Bobby Joe and she'd had just weeks before his disappearance, it surprised her that he hadn't changed his beneficiary. But then if he'd truly wanted to set her up for his murder, he would have left her name on the policy.

"I have no intentions of touching that money," she said.

Court stared at her, cursed under his breath, and he paused a long time. "I'm sorry about what happened yesterday when I tackled you like that. I was half crazy when I went out to your place."

That was true, but it was a craziness she could understand. She didn't get a chance to tell him that though because his phone rang, the sound shooting through the room. Her nerves were so frayed and raw that it caused her to gasp.

"It's Thea," he said when he glanced at the screen.

He knew the call could be important, and that was why Court answered it right away. He also put it on speaker.

"Your dad's awake," Thea stated, and with just those three words, Rayna could hear the relief in the deputy's voice. "He's still pretty groggy, but I thought you'd want to come and see him."

"I do." Court reached for his keys and his Stetson. He was already wearing his holster and weapon. But he stopped and looked at Rayna.

She could see the debate he was having. He didn't want to leave her there alone, but Court probably didn't want her near Warren, either. The debate didn't last long though.

"Rayna will be with me," he said to Thea. "What kind of security is in place at the hospital?"

"There's a guard posted outside Warren's door. Egan is there, too. And so is Griff."

Two lawmen and a security guard might not sound like a lot, but in this case, Warren was well protected.

"Good. We'll be there in fifteen minutes," Court assured Thea, and he ended the call.

Since it was normally about a twenty-minute drive from the McCall Ranch to town, Rayna guessed that they'd be hurrying. And they did. Court didn't waste any time getting her into the truck parked directly in front of the cabin, and they drove on the ranch road and then got onto the highway that led to McCall Canyon.

"It won't be a good idea for you to go into my father's room," Court said several minutes later, and he didn't give her a chance to disagree with that. "You can wait with Griff while I talk to him."

Court was right. She wanted to know if Warren had hired the dead PI, but he was far less likely to own up to anything with her in the room. Still, it wouldn't be a pleasant experiencing waiting with Griff. Yes, he would keep her safe, but he was firmly on the side of Warren when it came to anything, since Warren had practically raised Griff and his sister after their parents had been sent to jail for selling drugs.

"Keep watch," Court reminded her.

Even though she was already doing that, it caused her pulse to jump. The attack from the previous day was still way too fresh in her mind. Plus, she was having some pain, especially where the idiot had injected her with that drug. The seat belt was pulling right across the tender bruise.

"Are you okay?" Court asked.

He was frowning and glancing at her midsection. That was when Rayna realized she was holding her side. She was probably wincing, too. She nearly lied and told him everything was fine, but Rayna knew he wouldn't believe her.

"I'm hurting. I'm scared. And I'm mad. Yes, I messed up when I got involved with Bobby Joe. I should have never been with him in the first place, and I should have never stayed after the first time he hit me."

She wasn't sure how Court would react to that and expected him to dismiss it. He didn't. Even though he only glanced at her, she saw something in his eyes. Sympathy, maybe. If that was it, she didn't want it.

"I was a fool," she added. That not only applied to her relationship with Bobby Joe. She'd also been a fool to choose him over Court.

"Why exactly were you with him?" Court asked.

The burst of anger had come and gone, and now Rayna got a dose of something else that was familiar. Shame. There were plenty of emotions that came with the baggage of being in a relationship with someone like Bobby Joe.

"Because I didn't think I deserved anything better," she said. She certainly hadn't deserved Court.

He frowned. "What the heck does that mean?"

She hadn't expected him to understand. "You're a McCall from the right side of the tracks. You have a father and mother who love you." Rayna didn't have a clue who her father was, and her mother had dumped her at her grandmother's when Rayna had been in first grade.

Court's frown continued, and he added some profanity to go along with it. "You're telling you think you deserved to be with a jerk because you had some bad breaks in life?"

"I know it doesn't make sense to you." She looked at him. "It doesn't make sense to me now, either. I finally had, uh, well, an epiphany after Bobby Joe hit me the second time, and I knew if I stayed with him, the violence would only continue. Probably even get worse. That's when I ended our engagement." She paused. "And you know the rest."

Whether he believed the *rest* was anyone's guess, and there wasn't time to ask him. That was because he pulled to a stop in front of the hospital. He didn't use the parking lot. He left his truck by the curb, directly behind a cop car, and he hurried her inside.

Egan was right there to greet them.

One look at the sheriff's face, and Rayna knew something was wrong. She prayed that Warren hadn't had complications from the surgery. Or worse, that he'd died. She wasn't a fan of his, but she didn't want him dead. And that was partly because she knew how much Egan, Court and their sister, Rachel, loved him.

"What happened?" Court asked.

But Egan didn't respond. He made an uneasy glance around the waiting room, where there were several patients as well as some medical staff, and he motioned for Court and her to follow him. They did, and Egan went in the direction of the patients' ward, but he stopped in the hall. However, Rayna could see Rachel, Griff and Court's mother, Helen, just outside the door. It was no doubt Warren's room.

Egan looked at her as if trying to decide what to do with her. Clearly, he wanted to have a private conversation with his brother, but there was no way they could leave her alone.

"Dad didn't stay awake for long before he lapsed back into unconsciousness. But he did manage to say something," Egan said after he dragged in a long breath. He paused. "It's bad, Court."

And that was when Rayna heard something just up the hall. Something she didn't want to hear. Rachel and Helen were crying.

Chapter Five

Court had already had a bad feeling before he saw his mother and sister crying, but that feeling went up a significant notch.

"Is Dad..." But Court couldn't even bring himself to finish the question.

"He's alive," Egan assured him.

The relief came, but the bad feeling remained. That was because of the tense look on Egan's face.

"In the few minutes that Dad was conscious," Egan went on, "he kept repeating one thing. A woman's name. *Alma.*"

Court shook his head. "You think that's maybe the real name of the dead PI he supposedly hired?"

"No." Egan took in another of those breaths. "According to Griff, it's the name of dad's longtime mistress."

That bad feeling fell like an avalanche on

him. “No. Dad wouldn’t cheat on Mom,” he insisted.

“That’s what I said, too, but Griff says it’s true, that Dad’s been carrying on an affair with this Alma for thirty-five years. Dad recently broke off things with her though.” Egan turned back to Rayna. “And that’s where you come in. It’s possible this woman hired someone to kill Dad and set you up to take the fall.”

“Hell,” Court growled, and that was all he could manage to say.

His stomach was in knots. His heart, in his throat. And he figured Rayna wasn’t feeling exactly great right now to hear confirmation that someone had set her up to take the fall for his father’s attack. That part made sense—especially since they’d found Hallie dead. But none of the rest of this was sinking in.

“Alma,” Court repeated. He glanced at Griff. “And he is certain it’s true, that Dad cheated on Mom?”

Egan nodded, scrubbed his hand over his face. “He apparently found out a few months ago and said he told Dad to come clean. Dad obviously didn’t do that, but he did break off things with this woman.”

“The woman who maybe tried to set me up. I want to see her,” she insisted.

Egan nodded. "You will. I'll have her brought into the sheriff's office as soon as I can arrange it." He motioned toward Rachel and their mom. "Needless to say, they're upset." He paused again. "Griff also told me that Warren had a son with Alma. I didn't say anything about that to Mom."

Court hadn't figured there'd be any other shocks, but that certainly was one. All of this was coming at him too fast. Of course, this wasn't something he could absorb with just a conversation. And he was sure there would be backlash. How the devil could his father have done this?

"The son's name is Raleigh Lawton," Egan added a moment later. "He's a year older than you."

Court belted out another "Hell." Because he knew the man. *Sheriff* Raleigh Lawton was from a small town just one county over. Warren and he had worked on a murder case about three years ago, and Raleigh had visited McCall Canyon several times. Court thought of something else that'd happened.

"Wasn't Raleigh involved with Thea?" Rayna asked.

"Yes," Egan confirmed. "But they broke things off a while ago. I'm not sure if Thea knew he was Warren's son, but Griff says that Raleigh didn't know. He thought his father died in the military before he was born."

So, the lies had extended to not only their family but to Alma's, as well. Yeah, he definitely wanted to talk to this woman. Wanted to talk to his father, too.

"Are you okay?" Rayna asked. She touched his arm and rubbed gently.

No, he wasn't okay, not by a long shot, and Court figured things were about to get worse when he glanced at Rachel again. Griff had tried to put his arm around her, but Rachel practically pushed him away. She said something to their mom, something that Court didn't catch, and then his sister started toward Egan, Rayna and him.

"Egan told you?" she asked Court. There were fresh tears in her eyes and other tears spilling down her cheeks.

He nodded, tried to hug her, but Rachel waved him off. "I just need to get out of here. Away from Dad and away from Griff," she added. Her voice was shaking now. "He knew, and he didn't tell me."

"Maybe he didn't know how," Egan said.

"Then he should have found a way," she snapped. "He definitely should have found a way before—" She stopped, waved that off, too. "I need to go. Please. I just need to leave."

"I'll drive you," Egan volunteered. "Mom, too. Just wait here for a second until I can get her."

Egan started toward their mother, and Court went with him. Rayna stayed behind with Rachel. Which was good. As upset as the woman obviously was, she might try to leave on her own. If she did, at least Rayna could alert them. It wasn't safe for his sister to be out there alone.

Court went to his mother and pulled her into his arms. Unlike Rachel, she didn't push him away. She dropped her head on his shoulder.

"Warren loves me," Helen muttered. There was some anger in her voice now. "Why would he do this?"

Court didn't know, and he wasn't sure he'd get any answers from his father, either. "I'm sorry" was all he could think to say.

Griff was clearly sorry, too. The man was shaking his head and mumbling some profanity. Neither would help. But then, there wasn't much that could help this situation right now.

Helen pulled back and looked Court in the eyes. "You think that woman could have shot him?"

"Maybe," he admitted. "But we're looking

at Mitch for this, too. He hates Dad as well as the rest of us."

Still, if his father had hired that PI, then he must have believed that Alma could be some kind of threat.

"Mom, I want to take Rachel and you home," Egan insisted.

Helen didn't argue with that. She didn't look as if she had the strength to argue with anyone. In fact, she seemed broken.

"I'll stay here and help guard Warren," Griff offered. "Just tell Rachel that I'm sorry. I'm so sorry," he repeated to Helen.

But Court wasn't sure his mother heard Griff's apology. Even if she had, it wouldn't be nearly enough to help her get through this. Still, it hadn't been Griff's place to tell them. That blame was squarely on his father's shoulders.

Egan slipped his arm around Helen to get her moving, and Court followed them. "Why don't you take Rayna to the sheriff's office?" Egan told him. "I'll meet you there after I've driven Mom and Rachel to the ranch."

Court was still feeling stunned, but he forced himself to get moving. The sooner Rayna and he got to the sheriff's office, the sooner Egan and he could get Alma in for questioning. Not that Court was especially looking forward to meeting the woman, but this might be the start of getting those answers they desperately needed.

"Did you ever meet Raleigh or Alma?" Court asked Rayna as they walked toward the exit.

"No, but I remember the talk about Hannah Neal, the woman whose murder Warren and Raleigh were investigating. She was a surrogate who'd recently given birth, and she was killed around the same time Bobby Joe went missing."

Yeah. Hannah had been murdered in McCall Canyon, but her body had been dumped in Durango Ridge, Raleigh's jurisdiction. That was why both Raleigh and his father had been investigating it. All of that had happened just a few months before his father retired.

"You don't think Alma could have been connected to Hannah's murder, do you?" Rayna pressed.

He was about to say no, but then Court remembered that Warren had been very close to Hannah. She'd been the daughter of his best friend, a single-father cop who'd been killed in the line of duty. As Warren had done with Thea and Griff, he'd taken Hannah under his wing. So, maybe Alma had gotten jealous of that. After all, if she was the one who'd hired someone to shoot Warren, then it was possible she'd killed Hannah, too.

Yeah, he definitely needed to talk to this woman.

Egan led Rachel and their mother out the exit first, and he took them straight to his cruiser, which was parked just ahead of Court's truck.

"Will your mother be okay?" Rayna asked.

Good question. But Court wasn't sure. She'd already been teetering on shaky ground with Warren's shooting, and now this. Court made a mental note to call her doctor and have him go to the ranch to check on her.

He motioned for Rayna to follow him. However, before he could even get the doors unlocked, Court saw the blur of motion from the corner of his eye. And he immediately pulled Rayna down with him.

Just as someone fired a shot at them.

RAYNA HIT THE ground hard, much as they'd done the day before in her house, and the pain from the fall sliced through her. It robbed her of her breath.

For one heart-stopping moment, she thought she'd been shot.

But no, it wasn't that. The pain had come from the bruise on her side. It hurt, but it was far better than the alternative of having a bullet in her. Or in Court.

She checked to make sure he hadn't been hit. He didn't seem to be, but he dragged her beneath the truck and drew his gun. Ready to return fire.

Rayna took out her gun, too, from its slide holster. Not that she was in position to shoot back. She was on her stomach, and Court had positioned his body in front of hers.

Protecting her.

Something she wished he hadn't done. Rayna didn't want him to die because of her.

She waited, listening and praying. Rayna also tried to figure out what to do. If either Court or she reached up to open the truck door so they could get inside, the gunman could shoot them.

If there actually was a gunman.

There had only been the sound of that one shot, making her wonder if what they'd heard was a vehicle misfiring. That was what she wanted it to be anyway, and she hadn't actually seen a shooter.

"Call Egan and let him know what's happening," Court shouted out to someone. "But

I don't want him bringing my mother and sister back into this."

Rayna caught a glimpse of a medic in the doorway before the guy took out his phone and hurried back into the hospital.

"You're sure it's a gunman?" she asked.

But it wasn't necessary for Court to answer. She got confirmation of it when there was another shot. This one slammed into the back tire of the truck just inches from where they were. That caused her heart to skip a couple of beats because the bullet could have easily hit one of them. And now they had a flat tire, which would make it harder for them to drive out of there if they did manage to get inside the truck.

"Move," Court told her. He didn't wait for her to do that though. He pushed her farther beneath the truck. He also cursed. "I should have put you in the cruiser with Egan."

She wanted to remind him that hindsight was twenty-twenty and that he hadn't known this was going to happen. But there was no way Court would believe her. No, he would feel responsible for this.

Whatever *this* was.

Was it part of the earlier attacks against

Warren and her? Or maybe it was all connected to the two dead women?

They really did need to question Alma and find out if she was the one who'd hired this gunman. If she was, then it was possible that Rayna wasn't the primary target. Court could be. Because Alma could want to hurt Court to get back at Warren. That didn't mean either of them were safe though, and Court was the one taking most of the risks. He leaned out from beneath the truck, no doubt trying to see the gunman.

"Keep watch on your side," Court instructed.

Rayna was trembling, and still in pain, but she managed to get turned around so that her back was to Court's. And she immediately saw something. There were several people cowering by the sides of their vehicles.

"Stay down," she called out to them.

Another shot slammed into the truck. But the angle was different on this one than the other two. The gunman was moving. Court obviously realized that, too, because he cursed and shifted his position so that she could have a better view of the back of the truck.

"You see the gunman?" Rayna asked.

"No." But she immediately felt Court's muscles tense. “Yes,” he amended. “He’s directly ahead on the other side of a white car.”

Rayna could see the car but not the shooter. Not at first anyway, but then he came out from cover, fired a shot, and she got a glimpse of him then.

He was wearing a ski mask, and even though she hadn’t gotten a look at her attacker, Rayna sensed this was the same person. The build and height were right, anyway. But why did he want her dead now? He couldn’t set her up for Warren’s attack. Maybe he just thought she was a loose end, someone who could possibly ID him.

She couldn’t.

But maybe he didn’t know that.

The man leaned out again and fired another shot at them. This one slammed into the pavement and then ricocheted into the truck. Court rolled out from cover, too, and he sent two rounds the gunman’s way.

A sound on her right caught her attention, and Rayna pivoted in that direction. Not a gunman but a car. One that she recognized because it was Whitney’s. Her friend braked to a loud stop directly behind Court’s truck. That meant Whitney was now in the gunman’s line of fire.

"Hell, what is she doing?" Court grumbled. "She must have heard the shots."

Yes, there was no way to miss that. But maybe Whitney thought she could save them or something. If so, it wasn't a good plan because Whitney could be killed. Plus, it blocked their view of the gunman, making it impossible for them to return fire.

"Get in," Whitney called out to them.

Court and she couldn't do that, of course. It would be too risky for them to run to Whitney's car. If they were going to take that kind of chance, it would be better for them to just get in the truck, since it would take less time for them to be out in the open.

"Hear that?" Court asked her.

For a moment Rayna thought he was talking about Whitney. He wasn't. Because she heard another sound. It was a car engine. Since they were in a parking lot, it could just be someone leaving, but then there was the squeal of tires on the asphalt. Someone was driving out of there fast.

"He's getting away," Court said, and she could hear the frustration—and hesitation—in his voice.

Court no doubt wanted to go after the shooter, but it would be a huge risk. Because if it wasn't the gunman, then he could be shot. Still, he must have thought it was a chance worth taking because he rolled out from beneath the truck, his attention zooming to Rayna's right.

She lifted her head enough for her to see the car. It hadn't been the one the guy was using for cover though. This was a dark green sedan, and it was cutting across the parking lot only a few yards from them. Close enough for Rayna to catch just a glimpse of the ski-masked driver before he sped away.

"Stay put," Court warned her.

And with his gun aimed, he got to his feet and took off running.

Chapter Six

Court ran as fast as he could, and he kept his eyes on the green car. At best he figured he would get one shot before the shooter disappeared.

But he didn't even get that.

The car drove over the curb of the parking lot and shot out onto the road. Before Court could even stop and take aim, the gunman was already out of sight. That was not what he wanted. He needed to catch this guy so he could find out what the heck was going on.

While he ran back to Rayna, he took out his phone and texted Egan. His brother no doubt had deputies on the way, but Court wanted someone to go in pursuit of the person who'd just tried to kill them.

"Are you okay?" Rayna asked him the moment he made it back to her. She was crawling out from beneath the truck, but Court motioned for her to stay put. For a few more seconds, anyway. Just in case the shooter returned for a second round. Plus, he wanted a moment to ask Whitney one critical question.

"Why the hell did you drive into gunfire like that?" he snapped.

Whitney shook her head, her eyes widening. "I heard the gunshots and thought you needed some help."

He had. But not from a civilian. "You saw the gunman?"

Another shake of her head. "No. I only heard the shots."

Strange that most people's reaction would have been to move away from the gunshots. "You should have stayed back. Because you could have been killed." Well, she could have been if the shooter had continued to fire those shots. He hadn't. In fact, he'd stopped as soon as Whitney had driven up.

Her mouth trembled a little, and she looked as if she was about to cry. He hadn't wanted to bring her to tears—there'd already been enough of that today from his mom and sister—but he didn't want her doing anything like that again.

"You can't drive your truck on that flat tire," Whitney said. "And I don't think you want

Rayna staying out here any longer than necessary. Come on, I'll give you a ride to the ranch."

Normally, Court wouldn't have given it a second thought to agree to have Whitney take them to the station, but he was having a lot of second thoughts today. Maybe because he'd nearly gotten Rayna killed along with having his world turned upside down.

Court didn't have to decline because a cruiser pulled into the parking lot and came directly toward them. Thea was behind the wheel, and she lowered the passenger-side window as she came to a stop.

"Ian and John are going after the shooter," Thea said.

Both men were deputies with plenty of years wearing a badge. Maybe their experience and some luck would help them nab the gunman.

"Is she going with us?" Thea asked, tipping her head to Whitney.

"No." Court answered so fast that it had Rayna looking at him.

He decided to soften his tone a little when he turned to Whitney and continued talking. "Go home or wherever else you're headed. You shouldn't stay around here. I'll call you about coming in to give a statement."

Whitney went stiff as if displeased with that order. Maybe because she'd already told him that she hadn't seen the gunman, but people often remembered other details when questioned.

The moment Court got Rayna into the back seat of the cruiser, Thea took off. Rayna was still trembling, of course. She probably would for a while, and he found himself slipping his arm around her before he even realized he was going to do it. Worse, Rayna moved right against him as if she belonged there.

Not good.

The last thing Court needed right now was to let down the barriers between Rayna and him. It would cause him to lose focus, and besides, he didn't have time to deal with the old baggage that existed between them.

"Griff called and told me about Warren," Thea said, pulling his attention back to her. Like Court, Thea was also keeping watch all around them as she drove to the sheriff's office.

Court figured this conversation should wait, especially since he was only minutes out of a gunfight, but it was a subject he'd planned to discuss with Thea eventually. "Did you know about my dad's affair?"

He cursed Thea's hesitation, but he had to hand it to the deputy. She didn't dodge his gaze. She made eye contact with him in the rearview mirror. "I suspected. I accidentally overheard a conversation once between Alma and Warren. It seemed—" her gaze slid between Rayna and him "—intimate or something."

Court wanted to curse twice. Once because Thea had obviously picked up on the unwanted attraction between Rayna and him. He wanted to curse a second time because Thea should have told him about that conversation she'd overheard. Of course, she would have never done that. Thea was fiercely loyal to Warren and wouldn't have ratted him out. But that did lead Court to something else.

"You used to date Alma's son, Raleigh," Court said. And he waited.

Thea nodded. Paused. "Raleigh and Warren had a, uh, falling-out. I don't know about what. Maybe it involved the case of the dead surrogate they'd investigated together. Maybe because Raleigh learned the truth. Either way, it caused things to become tense between Raleigh and me, so we stopped seeing each other."

Court glanced at Rayna, and despite the

hell they'd just been through, he could tell she wanted more info from Thea.

"Is it possible Raleigh could be behind these attacks?" Rayna asked.

"No," Thea said without hesitation. "Even if he hated Warren, he's not the sort to bend the law, much less break it."

Court would have pressed for even more, but Thea pulled to a stop in front of the sheriff's office. She didn't get out though. She turned in the seat and looked at them. "As soon as I got Griff's call, I started asking around about Alma. I'd made some friends and contacts in Durango Ridge, where she lives. Anyway, last month Alma took some firearms-training classes."

That got his attention. "She has a permit for a gun?"

Thea nodded. "A permit to carry concealed." She blew out a frustrated breath. "You asked me if Raleigh could be behind this. No. But I can't say the same for his mother."

And that was why Court had to get Alma in for questioning. For now though, he didn't want to sit outside with Rayna any longer. He threw open the cruiser door and got her inside.

"I'm pretty sure Egan took your mom and Rachel straight home," Thea said when Court glanced around the nearly empty squad room. The only other person there was a reserve deputy, Dakota Tillman, and he was on the phone. "Griff's going to get someone to fill in for him guarding Warren, and then he'll come here."

Good. Griff wasn't a deputy, but it appeared they were going to be short of manpower for a while. Still, he didn't want Egan back here, not until he had Helen and Rachel safely back at the ranch. It wasn't a good idea for them to be in town with that shooter on the loose.

Since Rayna was still looking pretty shaky, Court took her to the small break room at the back of the building, and he got her a bottle of water from the fridge. While she made her way to the sofa, he called one of the deputies, Ian, for an update on the shooter. But Ian didn't answer. Hopefully, that was because he was making an arrest.

"If you want to go out looking for the gunman," Rayna said, "I'll be fine here."

No, she wouldn't be. She was probably close to having an adrenaline crash, and what he was about to tell her wouldn't make that better. "The shooter could come to the sheriff's office."

She inhaled a quick breath, almost a gasp. Yeah, that adrenaline crash was closing in on her. Court went to her, and keeping a safe distance away, he sank onto the sofa next to her.

"He probably won't come here," he added. "But right now, we don't know which one of us is his target. Either way, he'll probably guess this is where we'd go."

Rayna groaned, pressing the back of her head against the sofa. "If he does show up, at least one of us can shoot him. But if he gets away, he'll just regroup and come after us again."

Court couldn't argue with any part of what she said. That was all the more reason to find out the person behind this. Maybe that was Alma. Or Mitch. But there was someone else on Court's radar now.

"Do you think it's odd that Whitney showed up at the hospital when she did?" he asked.

That brought her head off the sofa, and she stared at him. "You think she could have put together an attack?" Her tone made it seem as if that would be impossible, but then she huffed. "What would be her motive?"

Court had to shrug. "You tell me. Are things solid between you two?"

"Yes." But Rayna hesitated. "No. They haven't been the same since Bobby Joe disappeared."

Court had picked up on that vibe, but he'd

wanted to hear Rayna confirm it. "Is that because Whitney believes you killed Bobby Joe?"

"Possibly," she admitted. "Whitney really liked Bobby Joe. She used to tell me how lucky I was to have him. Of course, that was before he hit me. After that, she didn't seem to be so much in his corner."

He gave that some thought. "Is it possible that Whitney had feelings for Bobby Joe, that maybe she could have been jealous of you?"

Rayna opened her mouth as if to deny that. She didn't. "Possibly," she repeated. "But it's a stretch to go from jealousy to attempted murder."

True, but jealousy could be a motive. "Bobby Joe's blood was in your house." Of course, she knew that, but Court wanted to look at this in a different light. "Blood that had been cleaned up."

"Yes, and the prosecution said I'd done that after I killed Bobby Joe. Since I didn't kill him, I'm guessing he put his own blood there and did the shoddy cleanup so that I would be arrested. But now you're suggesting that Whitney could have done that?"

"No. Just wondering if it's possible. Whitney would have had access to your house."

"At the time, so did Mitch." Rayna groaned

softly. "Besides, what's happening now might not even be connected to Bobby Joe. It could be happening because of Warren. If so, then Whitney couldn't be a suspect."

Maybe. But Court was going to keep her on the list just in case. Whitney not only had access to Rayna's place three years ago, she had access to it now. She could have possibly even gotten the code for the security system.

"I know this isn't comfortable for you." Rayna's voice was a rough whisper now. "It's okay if you put me in someone else's protective custody."

No. It wasn't okay. He refused to let their past play into this. "I'll do my job," he said, but he hated that it came out rough and edged with too much emotion. "Or rather I'll do my job better than I have so far. I nearly let you get killed."

"You nearly got yourself killed protecting me," she corrected. "I don't want anything happening to you because of me." That certainly wasn't a whisper, and she looked him in the eyes when she said it.

That riled him. And gave him an unwanted jolt of memories. Memories of what used to be between them. Memories of Rayna. She'd always been a little fragile. Probably because of her troubled childhood. And while she was trying her hardest not to look fragile now, she still was.

She continued to look at him as if she expected him to say that he would be pawning her off on someone else. But then her expression changed, and he saw something more than the feigned strength in her eyes.

Hell.

Rayna had almost certainly gotten a jolt of those memories, too.

Court didn't move. Neither did she. That wasn't good. Because he was thinking about doing something, like kissing her. Thankfully, his phone rang, and it was the reminder he needed that kissing should be the last thing on his mind. Especially when he saw Rachel's name on the screen.

"Are Rayna and you okay?" Rachel asked the moment he answered.

"Yes." That was probably a lie, but his sister had already had too much bad news. "How about Egan, Mom and you?"

Rachel gave a heavy sigh. "We're at the ranch, and the shooter didn't come after us. But Mom is, well, hysterical. Egan is with her now, but I had to call her doctor to come out here."

Court's stomach tightened. He wanted to

be there. No way though could he risk taking Rayna out into the open. "Tell Egan to stay there with her," Court instructed. "The other deputies are out looking for the shooter, and I have Rayna here at the station. Griff should be here soon."

Silence. Except it wasn't an ordinary silence. Rachel was obviously angry that Griff had known the truth about their father and hadn't told them. Court wasn't too happy about it, either, but he was going to cut the guy some slack on this. Yes, Griff should have told them, but the person who was at fault here was Warren. And now Helen might be falling apart because of what he'd done.

"I don't want to see Griff," Rachel added a moment later. "Please let him know he's not welcome at the ranch."

Court wanted to refuse to do that. After all, the McCall Ranch was Griff's second home, but he'd go with Rachel's wishes on this. Still, there seemed to be more going on that his sister wasn't saying.

"Is there something else you want to tell me?" Court came out and asked.

He got another round of silence from Rachel. "No. I just made a mistake with Griff, that's all. A big mistake."

Court definitely didn't like the sound of that. Griff and Rachel had been skirting around an attraction for years. Mainly because Warren hadn't thought they'd be a good match. But maybe something had happened. If they had indeed landed in bed without Griff telling Rachel the truth, then, yeah, it would have been a big mistake.

"Let me know if there's anything I can do," Court settled for saying. "And call me after the doctor has examined Mom. I'll be here if you need me."

He ended the call, and he glanced at Rayna. A reminder that Griff and Rachel weren't the only ones who'd been skirting attractions. Rather than sit there and continue to let the heat build, Court stood, ready to find out if there was any news on the search for the gunman. However, before he could do that, the break room door opened, and Thea stuck in her head.

"I just got off the phone with Alma Lawton," the deputy said. "She's on her way here now."

Good. That was a start. Now Court only hoped he could keep his emotions in check around the woman.

"Alma's not coming alone," Thea added a

moment later. "Her son and lawyer will be with her."

Court amended his earlier thought of "good." He figured he'd have enough on his plate just dealing with his father's mistress, but apparently that dealing was also going to include his half brother.

"If she's bringing her lawyer, Alma must realize she's a suspect in the attacks," Court pointed out.

Thea nodded. "She says she's innocent."

"Of course," Court grumbled, and he didn't take out the sarcasm. "Did she say anything else?"

Thea nodded again. "Alma says she has proof of who shot your father." Then Thea hesitated. "She says it was your mother."

Chapter Seven

Rayna had no trouble hearing what Thea had just said. And she supposed it wouldn't be much of a surprise that Warren's mistress was accusing his wife of attempted murder. Helen might be making the same accusations against Alma.

But Alma had to be wrong about this.

Judging from the way Court cursed, he felt the same way. "My mother didn't know about the affair until today, a day after my father was shot."

Thea held up her hands in a "you don't have to convince me" gesture. "Alma wouldn't say what kind of proof she had, but they should be here any minute." She stared at Court a moment. "You want me to be the one to interview her?"

It was a reasonable request, since it was obvious that Court wouldn't be objective about this, but Court shook his head.

"We need to keep everything by the book," Thea reminded him. "Remember, she'll have her sheriff son and her lawyer with her."

Yes, and they might be looking for anything they could use to have any possible charges dismissed against Alma. Court cursed again and then nodded. "I'll watch from the observation room."

Thea headed back toward the squad room, no doubt so she'd be there to "greet" Alma and her entourage. Court started there, too, but then he stopped and turned to Rayna. "You can watch the interview with me."

Rayna wasn't sure why Court was including her, but then if Alma was guilty of trying to kill Warren, then that meant Alma had also been the one to try to set Rayna up. She definitely had a vested interest in hearing what the woman had to say.

She thanked him and followed Court into the squad room just as the front door opened, and someone walked in. But it wasn't Alma.

It was Mitch.

Rayna groaned. She so didn't have the energy to deal with this hothead today. She braced herself for Mitch to start throwing insults and accusations their way, but he stopped in front of them, sliding his hands into his pockets. Court noticed what Mitch had done because he stepped protectively in front of her.

"I'm not armed," Mitch grumbled, but his comment didn't have his usually venomous tone to it. "I just wanted to find out if you'd learned anything new about Janet."

"No." Court huffed. "Rayna and I have been busy dodging bullets."

"I heard. And no, I don't know who it was doing the shooting." He also didn't sound the least bit concerned, either. "Like I said, I'm here about Janet."

Court stared at him a moment. "You seem awfully interested in this woman that you hardly knew. Is there something you didn't tell us about her?"

Now Rayna saw the familiar fire in Mitch's eyes. "I'm interested because someone murdered her. Just the way someone murdered my brother." He shifted his attention to Rayna. "I just want justice."

Court drew in a long breath before he answered. "I want justice, as well. But for that to happen, I need more information. And right now, you're the only person in town who seems to have known her."

"Your father did," Mitch quickly pointed out.

Court lifted his shoulder. "I haven't been able to confirm that. Right now, I'm more concerned about what you know about her. Were Janet and you *together* or something? And I'm not talking about chatting over coffee at the diner. Oh, and before you say no, I'll remind you that you said you saw her ID when it fell out of her pocket. I doubt she had that in her waitress uniform."

Mitch's eyes were already dark, and they stayed that way. "So? We were *together.* That doesn't mean anything."

"It means plenty," Court argued. "Since Janet was possibly the one who help set Rayna up, then she could have been working for her lover. *You.* Not my father. You could have been counting on Warren never waking up so that your secret would stay safe."

"There is no secret," Mitch said through clenched teeth. "This is just another case of the McCalls putting themselves above the law."

With that, Mitch turned to leave, but he practically stopped in his tracks when he saw the three people who were approaching the building. A dark-haired woman with a slender build flanked by two men. One was in a suit, and the other was dressed like a cowboy. A cowboy with a badge pinned to his chest.

This was no doubt Alma, her son, Raleigh, and her lawyer.

The corner of Mitch's mouth lifted, and he looked back at Court. "Things are about to get fun around here. Don't guess you'd let me stay for the show?"

"How do you know those people?" Court snapped.

Mitch blinked as if he'd said too much. "I don't. They just looked like the fun-causing sort." He strolled out, heading up the street away from their visitors.

"Mitch is lying," Court muttered. "I'll get him back in here after Alma's interview."

Rayna completely agreed with the lying part, and she watched to see if Alma or the men would have a reaction to Mitch. However, if they saw him, there didn't seem to be any signs of recognition. Of course, Alma wasn't exactly looking at Mitch. She had her attention zoomed right in on Court.

Raleigh opened the door, and Alma stepped in. She never broke eye contact with Court, but she swallowed hard. "I didn't expect you to look so much like Warren," she said, her voice a delicate whisper.

Actually, the rest of her looked delicate, too, with her pixie haircut and pale skin, and she was wearing a gauzy light pink dress. Rayna's first impression was that Alma looked much too young to have a son who was in his thirties.

Court ignored her observation and instead turned to Raleigh. Neither man said anything, but they seemed to be sizing each other up. Rayna did that as well, and she could see the strong resemblance. Both of them favored Warren.

She silently cursed. For Court's sake and the sake of his mother and sister, Rayna had been hoping this affair was all some kind of misunderstanding. Judging from his scowl, Raleigh had hoped the same.

"Sheriff," Court greeted.

"Deputy," Raleigh greeted back. "Who'll be interviewing my mother?"

"It won't be you," the guy in the suit said before Court could answer. "I'm Alma's lawyer, Simon Lindley."

Thea came forward and shook her head. "I'm Deputy Thea Morris, and I'll be doing the interview."

Raleigh and she exchanged a long look. The kind of look former lovers gave each other.

Rayna was certain she'd given Court that same look a time or two.

"I would have thought your brother, the sheriff, would have wanted to be here for this," Simon remarked.

"He's busy." Court's tone was as icy as his expression. "My mother isn't doing well, and my father is unconscious in the hospital. You might have heard someone murdered two women and tried to kill him." His gaze shifted to Alma when he added that last part.

Alma nodded. "Yes, I heard about Warren." She didn't offer any opinion about that and didn't ask how he was doing. The woman walked to Thea. "Perhaps we can go ahead and start?"

Simon looked as if he might stay and sling a barb or two at Court. He didn't. He hurried after Thea and Alma as they went up the hall to the interview room. Raleigh, however, stayed put.

"I'd like to listen," Raleigh said. "I suspect you'll want to do the same."

Court nodded and started for the observation room. Raleigh lagged behind and fell in step with Rayna. "You're a person of interest in Warren's shooting."

"Not anymore," Court answered before she

could say anything. "Rayna was being attacked and drugged at the time of the shooting, and she was miles away at her house. No. I'm looking more at your mother for doing this." Now there was some anger lacing his words.

"And my mother is accusing yours of doing the same." No anger in Raleigh's voice, but he did take in a weary-sounding breath.

"My mom didn't do this," Court insisted. "I don't care what Alma says because my mother had no idea my dad was cheating on her."

Raleigh made a sound that could have meant anything, and the three of them went into the observation room. In the interview room, Alma and Simon were having a whispered conversation. Thea was already at the table, waiting for them.

"Did you know about the affair?" Rayna came out and asked Raleigh. She wished she hadn't said anything though because Raleigh gave her a sharp look. Maybe because he thought she had no right to be here. But Rayna stayed put.

"No," Raleigh finally answered. His jaw clenched. "We raise horses, and apparently Mom was meeting Warren on her so-called business trips."

"And you didn't suspect?" Court pressed.

"No. Did you?" Raleigh fired back.

Even though they both had practically growled those responses, it seemed to bring them to some kind of truce. No, they didn't like what had been going on, maybe didn't even like each other, but they hadn't known this train wreck was about to happen. By now though, they probably knew plenty about each other. Rayna figured they'd both used their law-enforcement channels for some background checks.

"You're not going in the interview room with your mother?" Court added to Raleigh a few seconds later.

"No." He paused, and she could have sworn his jaw got even tighter. "I'm guessing you were upset when you learned about the affair." Raleigh didn't wait for Court to answer. "Now imagine if you found out you were born on the wrong side of the sheets to a man who hasn't acknowledged you or the affair for thirty-five years."

Court didn't actually jump to offer an opinion on that, but Rayna figured he could understand that Raleigh wasn't in a good place right now. He'd been lied to his whole life about his father, and now his mother was a murder suspect.

Yes, definitely not a good place.

The three of them turned their attention back to Thea once she began the interview. The deputy started with simple questions, asking Alma to state her full name and address. Rayna had been through enough interrogations to know what Thea was doing. She was establishing baseline responses of a potential suspect. Like many people, Alma's eyes went to the right when she answered truthfully. Now Thea had created a body-cue lie detector she could use for the harder questions.

And Thea jumped right into that.

"Tell me about your relationship with Warren McCall," Thea said.

"There is no relationship. Not any longer," Alma insisted. "We ended things two months ago."

"We?" Thea questioned. "Did you end it or did Warren?"

Alma glanced at Simon before she answered. "Warren. But it was time. All that sneaking around is fine when you're as young as you are, but I was tired of it. I wanted something more out of life. Something that Warren couldn't give me."

Thea jumped right on that. "So, you weren't upset when the breakup happened?"

Alma made another glance at her lawyer. "I

suppose I was. At first. But then I got over it. I certainly wasn't so enraged that I would plot to kill Warren."

"And it's ridiculous that you'd bring my client in for questioning about something like that," Simon added.

Thea ignored him, and she opened a folder she'd brought into the interview room. She extracted a photo of Hallie. Obviously, the woman was dead, and it caused Alma to gasp. Raleigh didn't have a verbal reaction to that, but Rayna could feel the tension practically flying right off him.

"Do you recognize her?" Thea asked.

"No." Alma closed her eyes and shook her head. She also dropped her head on Simon's shoulder.

"Showing her that wasn't necessary," Simon growled. "You could have just asked Alma if she knew the woman."

Thea ignored that, too, and she took out a second photo. This one was of Janet. "How about her?"

Simon slipped his arm around Alma as if to turn her away from the grisly picture, but Alma not only opened her eyes, she leaned in to have a closer look. "I know her. That's the woman who's been following me." Alma shifted her attention to Thea. "Who is she?"

"We're trying to confirm that now. When did she follow you?"

Alma huffed. "She's been doing it for the past couple of weeks. I got so worried that I took some firearms training."

Court turned to Raleigh to see if he would verify that, and Raleigh nodded. "She told me about someone following her, but I never saw the woman. You really don't know her identity?"

"Janet Bolin," Court answered after a long pause. "She was a PI."

Raleigh moved closer to the glass, staring at the picture. "Cause of death was a gunshot wound to the head." It wasn't really a question, but Court made a sound of agreement.

Even though Court didn't add anything about Warren possibly hiring the PI, it might make sense if Warren was concerned about how Alma might take the breakup.

Alma tapped Janet's picture. "She was carrying a gun the last time I saw her. I guess she thought it was concealed, but I could see the outline of it in the back waist of her jeans."

"Where and when did that happen?" Thea asked.

Alma's brow furrowed. "About a week ago,

maybe less than that. She was at the coffee shop in Durango Ridge." She paused a heartbeat. "Helen McCall was with her."

Court cursed and moved as if he might charge into the room, but Rayna took hold of his arm. She didn't remind him that Thea would get the info they needed, but Court must have remembered that he wouldn't be doing his mother or him any favors if he went in there and accused his father's mistress of lying.

Alma tapped the photo again. "This woman and Helen were talking. I know it was Helen because I've seen a photo of her in Warren's wallet. That's why I got so worried. I mean, my ex-lover's wife was chatting with an armed woman who'd been following me. And when I heard Warren had been shot, I figured these two had something to do with it. Specifically, I thought Helen had hired this woman to kill Warren."

Court cursed again. Obviously, this was hard to hear, and it wasn't making sense.

"I saw Helen minutes after she'd learned of the affair," Rayna said, "and she was genuinely upset. If she'd known for a week, those emotions wouldn't have been so raw."

Thankfully, Raleigh didn't argue with that,

but he probably wasn't as convinced of Helen's innocence as Rayna and Court were.

"Any idea why Helen McCall was in your hometown?" Thea asked the woman.

"I just assumed Warren had confessed all to her and that she was there to confront me or something. She didn't. And I never saw her again."

"You knew Helen was there?" Court asked Raleigh.

"No," he answered without hesitation. "But then if my mother had told me about Helen, she would have had to spill everything about Warren. It's my guess she wasn't ready to do that."

No, and Raleigh didn't seem happy about that, either. Alma's secret affair was also his secret paternity.

"Did Helen or Janet see you when you spotted them at the coffee shop?" Thea asked Alma.

Alma quickly shook her head. "But I went in through the side entrance and sat at a table on the other side of the wall from them. I couldn't hear much because it was noisy that day, but I did catch a word or two. They both mentioned Warren, of course. Oh, and a woman named Rayna."

That put a heavy feeling in her stomach,

and she exchanged glances with Court. Uneasy glances. Because why would his mother and a dead PI have been talking about her?

"What did the two women say about Rayna?" Thea pressed when she continued with the questioning.

"I didn't hear that part," Alma insisted, "only the mention of her name."

Rayna wanted to believe they were talking about someone else. Or maybe that Alma had just misheard. Heck, all of this could be a lie.

But it didn't feel like a lie.

Mercy, had Court's mother been the one responsible for all this violence?

"I'll call the ranch and talk to my mom," Court insisted. He took out his phone and stepped into the hall. However, it rang before he could press the number.

Rayna was close enough to see Griff's name on the screen, and that put some fresh alarm in Court's eyes. He answered it on the first ring.

"Is something wrong?" Court immediately asked.

"Yeah," Griff answered. "Someone just tried to kill Warren."

Chapter Eight

Court's first reaction was to jump into a cruiser and head straight to the hospital. Someone was trying to kill his father—again.

His dad was in danger.

But Court forced himself to stop and think. This could be some kind of trap. Not for his father but for Rayna and him.

"Is Dad okay, and who tried to kill him?" Court asked Griff.

"Warren's fine. As for the intruder, I'm not sure who he is, yet, but we did stop him before he could actually get into the hospital room. I just cuffed him. But I can't take him anywhere because I don't want to leave Warren with only the security guard."

Neither did Court. He glanced around to see if he could come up with a solution. There were only two deputies in the sheriff's office, and

Thea was still questioning Alma. The other deputies were out chasing down the shooter.

"We should go to the hospital," Rayna insisted.

Considering they'd just been attacked there, it surprised him that she would be so accommodating, but maybe Rayna didn't like the idea of staying behind with Alma. Court didn't like that, either.

"I'll be there in a few minutes," Court told Griff, and he ended the call.

Court turned to Raleigh, not sure of what he should say to the sheriff. Not sure what Raleigh would say, either. He'd likely heard what Griff had said and now knew that there'd been another attempt on Warren's life. However, if Raleigh had any reaction to that, he didn't show it.

"If you don't question your mother about what you've just heard in the interview," Raleigh said, "then I'll request the Texas Rangers do it. Helen McCall needs to explain why she was talking with a now dead person of interest in this case."

It bothered Court that Raleigh was dictating to him how to do his job, but at this point anything the man said or did would probably bother him. There wasn't much about this situation that Court liked.

"I'll question my mother," Court assured him. Though it probably would be smart to have a Ranger do it. Not Griff, either. But someone who could be objective about all of this. Of course, his mother might not be in any shape to hold up to a full-blown interrogation.

Raleigh nodded, tipped his head to Alma. "I'm sure Thea will call you if there are any problems with the rest of the interview," he added.

It was pretty much a blanket invitation for Court to leave, so that was what he did. He took Rayna by the hand, hurried her to a cruiser that was just outside the door, and he prayed they wouldn't be shot at along the way.

Court's phone rang again, and this time he saw Rachel's name on the screen. He took the call on speaker, tossing his phone on the seat so his hand would be free. Court also kept watch around them, something that Rayna was doing, as well.

"Egan just told me about Dad," Rachel said the moment she was on the line.

"Yeah. I don't know anything yet, but I'll be at the hospital soon." Court debated if he should even bring this up now, but it was a conversation that needed to be started. "Once I'm sure Dad is okay, I'll need to talk to Mom. Alma Lawton said some things about her during her interview."

Rachel groaned. "I hope you don't believe anything Dad's mistress would have to say."

In this case, he did believe her. Either that or it was a stupid lie on Alma's part, since his mother's meeting with Janet was something that could be easily verified. Well, easily if his mother wasn't coming unglued.

"I just need to talk to Mom," Court settled for saying. "I'll call you when I have info on the intruder. All I know right now is that Griff was able to stop him, and he's still with Dad right now."

"Griff," Rachel repeated like profanity. "Call me the minute you know anything."

Court assured his sister that he would, ended the call and pulled to a stop in front of the hospital entrance. As close as he could, anyway. The CSIs were there, and so were several Texas Rangers. Obviously, that was Griff's doing, and Court made a mental note to thank him.

He threaded Rayna through the crime scene tape and got her into the building as fast as possible. There was another Ranger posted just inside, and the waiting room had been cleared. Good. The fewer people, the better.

"No way would your mother have done something to put you in danger," Rayna said as they walked.

Court believed that, too, but there might be another side to this. If Helen had found out about the affair sooner than she had let on, she could have wanted to harm Warren. Court hated to even consider it, but it was something he had to do. It sickened him though to think his mother might have had any part in this.

The moment they were in the patients' hall, Court spotted Griff and the security guard, David Welker, someone who Court knew and trusted. He also saw the man they had on the floor. The guy was on his stomach, his hands cuffed behind his back.

"How's Dad?" Court asked Griff first off the bat.

"Still unconscious."

That was better than the alternative or his father being bedridden and aware that someone had come back to finish him off.

Court looked down at the intruder. So did Rayna, but she shook her head, indicating that she didn't know him. Neither did Court, but he pulled the man to his feet so he could have a face-to-face talk with him. Except it wasn't really a man. The guy looked to be a teenager, but he was also dressed like an orderly.

"Did he have any ID on him?" Court asked Griff.

"No. The only thing in his pocket was this." He took out a small Smith & Wesson handgun. "He doesn't work here. The badge he's wearing is a fake."

The badge looked real enough, but something must have alerted Griff. "What made you stop him from going into Dad's room?"

"A bad gut feeling. That, and he looked too young to be an orderly."

He did, and Court thanked Griff before he turned back to the kid. "Who are you?" Court demanded.

The kid lifted his head, making eye contact with Court, and the deputy cursed. "He's high on drugs or something."

"That was my guess, too," Griff agreed.

The corner of the kid's mouth lifted. "I only had a pill or two." His words were slurred, as well.

"Who are you?" Court repeated, and this time he got right in the guy's face. His scowl must have been mean-looking enough because it caused the kid's smile to vanish.

The kid shook his head. "You don't know me. My name won't mean anything to you." He glanced over Court's shoulder at Rayna. "Might mean something to her though."

Rayna went stiff. "I have no idea who he is."

The kid shrugged. "Figured you would, since you're the one who hired me to come here and all."

"I didn't," Rayna snapped, and she repeated it, her gaze volleying between Court and Griff.

Court grabbed on to the guy's shirt, and the last scowl was a drop in the bucket compared to the one he gave him now. "I want to know your name."

"Bo Peterson," he finally answered.

That meant nothing to Court, and judging from Rayna's reaction, it meant nothing to her, either.

"When did I supposedly hire you?" Rayna demanded.

"Yesterday morning. You were wearing a red dress then."

Rayna groaned. "Hallie hired him."

"She said her name was Rayna." Bo leaned in, blinking and trying to focus on her face. "But you don't talk the way she did. And you don't look the same."

"Because she's not that woman," Court fired

back. "In fact, that woman is dead. Someone murdered her and a second woman. Since you just tried to kill my father, you're my number one suspect in those killings and several attacks. That means you could get the death penalty."

Bo's eyes widened, and he suddenly looked a lot more alert than he had just a few minutes ago. "I didn't kill anyone. And I wasn't supposed to kill the person in that room. I was to put the gun behind the toilet."

Court's stomach tightened. That meant someone planned to retrieve the gun later and use it. Probably on Warren. Of course, that would have happened only if Bo was telling the truth. Court wasn't anywhere near convinced of that yet.

"I didn't kill anyone," Bo said when Court, Rayna, David and Griff just stared at him.

"Even if you didn't, you're still an accessory to murder and attempted murder. That carries the same penalties."

"No," Bo practically shouted. "I didn't know anyone was going to get killed." He snapped back toward Rayna. "That other woman is really dead?"

She nodded. "And that's why you have to tell us everything you know about her."

"I don't know anything." He shook his head and tears watered his eyes. "Several times she told me her name was Rayna."

She'd done that no doubt so Bo would remember it. "What else did she say, and how did she pay you?"

"She paid me in drugs. Oxy and Ecstasy. But I screwed up. I was supposed to put the gun in the room yesterday, but I took some of the pills and got a little messed up."

"What time yesterday?" Court pressed.

Bo's forehead bunched up, and he groaned. "Around nine or so. She didn't know what room number. She said I was to find out what room number Warren McCall was in and plant it there."

So, maybe Hallie had met with Bo shortly after the shooting. That would have meant he was perhaps the last person to see her alive. Of course, Bo could have also been the one to kill her.

"Who was going to use the gun you were supposed to hide behind the toilet?" Court continued.

"She didn't say, and I didn't ask."

That last part didn't surprise Court. Bo had likely been in a hurry to down those drugs he'd been given as payment.

"Can I go now?" Bo asked.

Court didn't even bother to laugh and he looked at Griff. "Any chance one of your Ranger friends can drive this clown to the sheriff's office so he can be locked up?"

"Locked up?" Bo howled. "But I didn't do anything. I didn't even make it into the old man's room."

Yeah, thanks to Griff and David. That was why Court had to continue to make sure whoever had hired Hallie and Bo wouldn't send someone else to try to finish off Warren.

"I'll wait in your dad's room," David said when Griff led Bo away.

Court thanked him and took out his phone to call Rachel and Egan, but first he looked at Rayna to make sure she was okay. She wasn't. She was looking shaky again, so he had her lean against the wall.

"Who's trying to set me up?" she muttered, but it didn't seem as if she expected him to answer. Good thing, too, because Court still didn't know.

Court pulled her into his arms, intending for it to be just a quick hug, but it didn't stay that way. That was because Court realized Rayna wasn't the only one who'd just felt as if the rug had been pulled out from beneath them.

"Bobby Joe," she said. "He's the only one who hates me enough to do this."

Maybe. But this might not be about Rayna. "Or you're the perfect scapegoat because of the bad blood between you and the McCalls."

Of course, at the moment that bad blood didn't look so bad. After all, Rayna was in his arms, and when she lifted her head and looked up at him, it put their mouths much too close together. The memories came. The good ones. Of other times when he'd kissed her and she'd responded.

Much like she was responding now.

Her breath kicked up a notch, and he could see her pulse fluttering in her throat. And he caught her scent. Something warm and silky. Definitely nothing that had come from a bottle, and it stirred him in a very bad way. That was why Court stepped back before he made a mistake both Rayna and he would regret.

Well, they'd regret it afterward anyway.

He was certain there wouldn't be much of anything but pleasure during the actual kissing.

"We keep doing that," she said.

He didn't ask her to clarify. Because he knew. They kept moving much too close to giving in to this heat. That reminder caused him to take yet another step away from her, and before he could go back and play with fire, he made that call to Rachel. But it wasn't his sister who answered.

It was his mother.

"Rachel left her phone by my bed when she went to make me some tea," his mother said. "She won't be long though. Is everything okay? Egan and she are whispering."

Court wanted to assure her that everything was okay. But it wasn't. Far from it. "Dad is still asleep," he said.

"I guess that's good. He probably needs to rest and heal. If Warren really did do this to me, then I can't forgive him."

"Just give it some time," he said, because Court didn't know what else to say.

"Time won't fix this. I'm sorry," she added. "They gave me some pills, and they've made me a little woozy. Did you want me to get Rachel for you?"

"No, I need to talk to you." And because he had no choice, Court had to pause and take a deep breath. "We brought Alma Lawton into the sheriff's office for questioning."

"I see." His mother paused, too. "Did she know about me?"

Court went with the truth on this. "Yes. She also admitted to the affair."

Another sob. "Oh, God. It's true."

"According to Alma. But you still need to talk to Dad about it." In fact, Court definitely wanted to hear a confession from his father's own mouth, and part of him wouldn't fully believe it until he heard it.

"No, I can't talk to him. If Warren did have an affair with that Alma, then he had a child with her. A son."

Court was a little surprised that his mother could put all of that together—especially considering she'd been given those sedatives. It also made him wonder who'd told Helen about Raleigh. Maybe she'd overheard it in one of those whispered conversations she'd mentioned.

"Yes, they possibly had a son," Court admitted, but he didn't give her a chance to ask him any more about that. He jumped right into his question. "Alma said you had coffee with a woman named Janet in Durango Ridge. Did you?"

"No. I don't know a Janet." She didn't pause that time.

Court felt the relief. He could see that relief in Rayna's eyes, too, since she was still close enough to hear the phone conversation. But the relief didn't last because Court knew that Janet might not even be the PI's real name.

"Did you meet with a woman in Durango Ridge?" Court pressed.

"Yes."

There went the rest of his relief. At least his mother hadn't denied it, and that meant he might be able to get the truth from her. He only hoped the truth didn't lead to her arrest.

"I met with a reporter named Milly Anderson," Helen added a moment later. "She said she was working on the old Hannah Neal murder case. You know, the one that's troubled your father for the past three years."

There was no need for his mother to add that last sentence. Because Court definitely knew about Hannah's case. Her murder was still unsolved. "Why did Milly want to talk to you about Hannah?" Court asked.

"Because she's an investigative reporter. You know, one of those journalists who digs through cold cases. She didn't really have anything new. I guess she thought maybe I would remember something that would help her."

Court doubted that. No, Janet or whatever her name was had probably had a different agenda in mind. Court just didn't know what that was.

"Did you tell Dad about this chat with Milly?" Court continued.

"I mentioned it to him. He said I shouldn't talk to any other reporters, that Hannah's murder was a police matter. He seemed really angry or something. God," she quickly added, "you don't think Milly had anything to do with Alma, do you?"

Court intended to find out. That meant digging more into Alma's background and talking to Raleigh. He might have run into Milly, as well.

"Oh, here's Egan," his mother said. "He's motioning to talk to you."

"I just got off the phone with Thea," Egan explained the moment he came on the line. "She told me what Alma said. You asked Mom if it was true?"

"Yes, she met with Janet in Durango Ridge."

Egan cursed, causing their mother to scold him, and Court heard footsteps, letting him know that Egan was taking this conversation out of Helen's earshot.

"Janet told Mom she was a reporter," Court added when he could no longer hear his brother moving around. "How is Mom, by the way?"

"Upset. Dr. Winters wants her to have a psych eval, and he's set her up an appointment."

That caused his chest to tighten. "You think she needs that?"

"Yeah."

Court wished he'd heard some doubt in Egan's voice. He didn't.

"I'll keep you posted on that," Egan went on. "In the meantime, the CSIs tested the guns at Rayna's house, and none had been fired recently. That's good news. For her, anyway."

Yes, it was, and while Court figured that pleased her, it also wasn't a surprise. Rayna had been adamant from the start that she hadn't fired a weapon. Especially one aimed at Warren.

"Thea said other than Mom's meeting with Janet, she didn't get much else from Alma," Egan continued. "Alma did agree to have her hands tested for gunshot residue. There wasn't any. And she also said the CSIs could test the weapons she owned."

Court was betting those wouldn't be a match, either. If Alma had been behind the attacks, she wouldn't have used her own gun. And she would have taken precautions to make sure there was no residue.

"What's going on between Rayna and you?" Egan came out and asked.

The question threw Court. It threw Rayna, too, because her eyes widened in surprise.

"What do you mean?" Court grumbled.

"You know what I mean. Are you two involved again? And no, it's not just me being nosy. I don't care who you take to your bed. I just want to make sure you're not sleeping with a woman who's neck deep in a murder investigation."

"I'm not sleeping with her." Though Court had thought about it. Those thoughts had come shortly after their near kiss. Heck, they were still coming now.

"Good. I just wanted to make sure you hadn't lost your mind." Egan paused. "I'm guessing Rayna thinks Bobby Joe is responsible for the attacks."

"Yes," she answered.

Egan didn't seem surprised that Rayna had been close enough to Court to hear what they were saying. "I figured as much. Of course, I don't believe it, but I'll take a harder look at Mitch. Once this situation with Mom is settled." And with that, Egan ended the call.

"I'm sorry," Rayna said. "I probably shouldn't have let Egan know I was listening."

"He already knew." Court wished that weren't true, but Egan was definitely aware of the attraction between Rayna and him. Aware, too, of the problems that it could cause.

"Let me check on my dad, and we can go back to the station," Court told her. "I want to question Bo."

He opened the door to his father's room and came face-to-face with David. "I was just coming to get you." The guard stepped back. "Your father's awake."

Chapter Nine

Rayna stopped in her tracks after hearing what the guard said to Court. *Your father's awake.* That meant Court was finally going to get to question Warren about the affair and the attack, and he almost certainly wouldn't want her there to hear it.

Or so she thought.

Court motioned for her to follow him. "It'll be safer in here. Bo might not have been working alone."

That caused her throat to snap shut, and she wondered why that hadn't already occurred to her. It was because there was a tornado of emotions going on in her head right now. In her heart, too. But Rayna tried to push all of that aside for the possible firestorm they were about to face.

"I'll let the nurses know he's conscious," David said, heading out into the hall.

"Dad," Court greeted. "You know why you're here in the hospital?"

Warren nodded. "Someone shot me."

Rayna stayed back against the wall as Court walked to his father's bed. She'd hoped that Warren wouldn't even noticed her.

He did.

Warren looked past Court and directly at her. Court followed his father's gaze and shook his head. "Rayna's not the one who tried to kill you."

"No. But it looks as if someone tried to kill her." He'd no doubt seen the injury on her head before Warren's attention shifted to Court. "I know you'll ask, but I didn't see the person who shot me."

Too bad. Rayna was hoping they could have cleared all of this up right now.

"I felt the bullet go into my chest." Warren touched that part of his body. "I fell, and the only thing I remember after that is bits and pieces of conversations I've heard from the nurses and guards."

"What did you hear?" Court pressed.

Warren groaned softly and closed his eyes for a moment. "That there was another attack. Are you two okay?"

"Fine." Court sounded disappointed. And

probably was. If that was all his father could recall, then there was going to be a lot more information they'd need to gather. "What about you? Are you in much pain?"

Warren shook his head, but that was probably a lie, since the head shake caused him to wince a little. That was the only reaction he managed to have, because the door flew open and one of the nurses came in. Rayna knew the woman, Ellen Carter, and she made a beeline to Warren, immediately checking one of the monitors.

"I'll let the doctor know you're awake." Ellen glanced at both Rayna and Court. "I know you'll want to question him about the shooting, but don't overdo it."

Court nodded but didn't say anything. Neither did Warren until the nurse was out of the room. "How's your mother? Is she here?"

"Not at the moment." Court didn't pause too long before he said that. "She's at the ranch with Rachel and Egan."

"Egan," Warren repeated. "Yes, he should be with her. Rachel, too." He looked up at Court again. "Do you have the person who shot me in custody?"

"No." Court took a deep breath. "But we have two dead bodies. Both women. One was an actress that we believe was posing as Rayna to set her up to take the blame for your shooting. The second one was perhaps a PI who was linked to you. She was using the name Janet Bolin."

For a man who'd just again regained consciousness after surgery, Warren suddenly seemed very alert. And frustrated. Because he groaned. "That's not her real name. It's Jennifer Reeves."

She couldn't see Court's face, but he did pull back his shoulders. If Warren knew the woman's real name, then he was indeed linked to her.

"You said she's dead?" Warren questioned.

"Murdered," Court clarified.

Warren grimaced and then cursed. "How? Did the person who shot me also kill her?"

"We're still trying to sort that out." Court dragged up a chair and sat next to his father's bed. "After surgery, you kept saying someone's name. Alma."

And the silence began. However, Warren did have a response. The shock, followed by a mumbled "Ah, hell."

That probably wasn't what Court wanted to hear. Maybe he had still held out hope that the affair was some kind of misunderstanding.

Warren looked Court straight in the eyes. "Your mother knows?"

Court nodded. "We all know. Griff filled in a few blanks for us."

Warren's mouth tightened. "He had no right. If I'd wanted all of you to know, it should have come from me."

"But it didn't," Court quickly pointed out. There was anger in his voice. Understandably so. That "if" probably didn't set well with him, and it meant that Warren hadn't planned on confessing to the affair anytime soon.

"That's why your mother's not here," Warren added. He also added some more profanity. "Call her now. Tell her I want to see her."

"That's not a good idea." Court didn't break eye contact with Warren when he said that, either. "The doctor sedated her, and she needs some rest."

Warren threw back the covers as if to get up, but Court quickly stopped him. "You need your rest, too. And I need answers. You really had an affair with Alma Lawton for thirty-five years?"

Warren stared at him almost defiantly. Obviously, he wasn't a man accustomed to being challenged, but Rayna saw the exact moment he mentally backed down. Warren stared at his hands. "What else do you know about her?"

Rayna wanted to groan. Even now after he'd been caught, Warren wasn't ready to spill everything.

"I know Alma gave birth to your son Raleigh," Court readily answered. "And that you and Alma only ended things a couple of months ago. I believe you were concerned Alma might go to Mom, and that's why you hired the PI." He paused. "How am I doing so far?"

Warren's mouth tightened even more. "Alma and I didn't end things. I did. I stopped seeing her, and she was upset about that. So, yes, I thought she might go to your mother."

"Why would Jennifer aka Janet meet with Mom in Durango Ridge?" Court pressed.

Warren lifted his head. "She wouldn't have."

"She did. Or rather according to Alma, they did. She said she saw them at a coffee shop there."

"You've already talked to Alma?" Warren snapped.

"Thea interviewed her. You have to know that she's a suspect. You really think she could have been the one to shoot you though?"

"No." But Warren immediately shook his head. "Alma's never done anything violent before."

That didn't mean she hadn't done this. It depended just how riled Alma was. Warren's scorned lover could have shot him, set up Rayna to take the fall, and when that didn't work, she could have hired someone to shoot at Court and her.

But that still didn't explain why the PI that Warren had hired would meet with Helen.

The door opened, and the doctor came into the room. He no doubt noticed the agitation on his patient's face because he huffed and turned to Court. "I need to examine Warren now. You two can wait out in the hall."

That definitely had a "get out of here" tone to it, and Rayna couldn't blame him. Yes, Warren had messed up big-time, but he was still in serious condition. Just a day earlier, he'd been at death's door, and the doctor probably wanted to give Warren some time to mend.

Court and she went out of the room, and he immediately took out his phone. He pulled up Egan's number, but he didn't press it. Court just mumbled some profanity and looked at her.

"I'll get you out of here soon," he said.

She got the feeling that he'd wanted to say something else. Maybe an apology or something. She didn't want one. Because none of this was his fault, and it was obvious that what his father had done was tearing him apart.

Court stared at her a moment longer before he finally pressed Egan's number, and this time he put the call on speaker. Court opened his mouth, probably to tell Egan that Warren was awake, but Egan spoke before he could speak.

"Mom swallowed a bunch of pills," Egan blurted out. "I've already called an ambulance, but she's unconscious."

Oh, mercy. Not this. Court and his family already had enough on their plates.

"When did this happen?" Court snapped.

"I'm not sure. Rachel's the one who found her. Are you still at the hospital?"

"Yeah. Dad is finally awake. I'll talk to you about it when you get here. You are coming in the ambulance with Mom, aren't you?"

"I am, but I'm not sure they'll keep her there. Once they've pumped her stomach or whatever the hell it is they'll do, she'll probably have to go to a place that has a psych ward."

Court groaned, scrubbed his hand over his face. "I'll meet you at the ER. How soon before you get here?"

"Soon. The ambulance is already on the way out here."

Still, that could be a good thirty minutes

by the time the medics picked up Helen at the ranch and brought her in.

Court got them moving when he ended his call with Egan. Maybe because he needed to put some breathing room between his father and him. Also, he might not want to have to tell Warren about this.

He stopped just short of the ER waiting room, and they peered around the corner. The Rangers were still there, so hopefully that meant a gunman wouldn't be stupid enough to show up there.

"I'm sorry," Court said.

Since she was about to tell him the same thing, Rayna lifted her eyebrow. "For what?"

"Everything. You could be in the middle of this danger because of my father's affair." He didn't say the word *father* with too much affection. However, there was plenty of anger. "I can't believe he did something like this."

After everything Warren had put her through with the trial, Rayna wanted to say that she had indeed thought he was capable. But yes, even she was surprised. Warren could be a bulldog when it came to seeking justice, but he'd seemed to genuinely love his wife and family. And now he was tearing them apart.

"If my mom dies..." Court started.

But Rayna didn't let him finish that. She stopped him by brushing her mouth over his. In hindsight, kissing him hadn't been the right thing to do. But it certainly caused the heat to slide right through her.

She leaned back, their gazes connecting, and this time she saw more than the worry and fatigue. There was some confusion. And a little fire.

"Have only good thoughts about your mother," she warned him. "Or I'll kiss you again."

Despite everything going on, the corner of his mouth lifted. "Not much of a threat." But then he huffed, and she understood what he meant.

In some ways, kissing was the greatest threat of all.

And that was why she stepped back. Just like that, the moment was lost, taking the fire right along with it. Unfortunately, Rayna knew it would return.

His phone rang, and since he still had it in his hand, she had no trouble seeing the screen. Not Egan this time but rather Thea. He put this one on speaker, too.

"How's Warren?" Thea immediately asked.

"Awake. He confirmed the affair with Alma."

"I see." Thea sounded very disappointed

about that. "Griff is here with the prisoner. I'll send the gun he had on him for testing. Anything specific you want me to look for?"

"Fingerprints or some DNA," Court answered. "It's possible this gun was going to be used to set someone up."

He looked at Rayna then, and she knew the someone might be her. She didn't remember touching a gun that wasn't hers, but it was possible someone had gotten a sample of her DNA.

"I finished the interview with Alma," Thea added a moment later.

"Yeah, Egan told me."

"Figured he had. Alma will be back tomorrow though to go over her statement. If you or Egan wanted to question her, you could do it then."

Court made a sound of agreement. "We don't have any grounds to arrest her. Not yet. But I need to look into her possible connection to the dead PI. According to my dad, her real name is Jennifer Reeves. And yes, he did hire her. Can you see what you can pull up on her?"

"Sure." And Rayna could hear the clicking of the computer keys. "Alma said Jennifer met with your mother. Do you know why?"

"No idea, and it might be a while before I

can ask her." Judging from the sudden tightness in his jaw, that was all he wanted to say about that right now.

"Jennifer Reeves," Thea repeated a moment later. "Yes, she was a PI. Thirty-four. No record. She owns...*owned* an agency in San Antonio but didn't have any other employees. Let me check her social media and see if I find any connection to Helen."

"And check connections to Alma, too," Court insisted.

"You think Alma could have been lying?"

"I don't know, but if Alma is on some kind of vendetta, then she might have used Jennifer to do it. Alma could have found out my father hired Jennifer and then paid her more money to set him up."

Yes, because after all, it'd been Jennifer who'd taken the photo of the woman who resembled Rayna. But then Rayna thought of something else.

"Maybe you'll find a connection between Jennifer and Mitch," Rayna threw out there.

Thea made an immediate sound of agreement. "There did seem to be something going on between those two, and Mitch is definitely someone who'd want to get back at Warren and you." She paused. "I'm not seeing anything on her social media, but I'll see about getting her case files. It's possible… Oh."

Rayna definitely didn't like the sound of that "oh." Thea wasn't exactly the sort to be easily surprised.

"What is it?" Court asked when Thea didn't continue.

"I think we should be looking into someone else," Thea finally said. "I'm sending you a photo that I found on Jennifer's page. You want me to bring her in for questioning?"

It took a few seconds for the photo to load on Court's phone. It was a shot of two women, and they appeared to be at some kind of party. When Rayna looked at their faces, it felt as if someone had drained all the air from the room.

The woman on the left was definitely Jennifer. But Rayna recognized the other woman, too.

Because it was Whitney.

Chapter Ten

Court definitely didn't like this latest turn of events. Why the heck had Whitney not mentioned that she knew Jennifer?

From all accounts Jennifer had been working at the diner for a couple of weeks, and Whitney lived in town. As small as McCall Canyon was, she would have likely run into her, seen her friend and then been very concerned that her *friend* had turned up dead. The very friend that from all appearances had tried to set up Rayna for a crime she didn't commit.

Court drove away from the hospital while Rayna tried to call Whitney. They were alone in the cruiser but not alone on the road. He hadn't wanted to risk that. Deputy Dakota Tillman and a Texas Ranger were in a second cruiser behind them, and Court hoped that three lawmen would be enough to deter another attack.

"Whitney's still not answering her phone," Rayna said. It was her fifth attempt to get in touch with the woman, but each of the calls had gone straight to voice mail.

Court figured that wasn't a good thing no matter which way they looked at this.

"You think it's possible Whitney got wind that you learned she was connected to the dead PI?" Rayna asked.

"Yeah," he admitted. Since Whitney was a dispatcher for the sheriff's office, she could have heard and might now be avoiding them.

Or…

There was another possibility. One that he didn't want to mention to Rayna just yet. If Whitney had gotten involved in some kind of scheme to kill Warren, a scheme that involved Jennifer and Hallie, then she could be dead, too.

"I keep going back to what Whitney did earlier in the hospital parking lot," Rayna said. "She pulled her vehicle between us and the shooter."

Whitney had indeed done that, and while that alone wasn't an indication of guilt, she was starting to look very suspicious. "I'll question Whitney as soon as she checks in with us."

And the woman had better do that soon. She'd also better have the right answers.

Rayna glanced at the sheriff's office as they drove past. "You can leave me there if you want, and go back to the hospital and be with your mother."

"Rachel and Egan are there, and the doctor said he didn't want her to have visitors for a while. Even if she were allowed, I'm not sure I should be answering questions she'll have about my dad's affair. It would only upset her even more."

It had certainly upset Court. And worse, he didn't know what to do about it. Part of him hated his father for this, but hating wasn't going to fix the danger. Or his mother. No. He had to focus on getting the person responsible for the attacks and then make sure his mom had the kind of help she needed to get better.

His phone dinged with a text message, and Court handed it to Rayna so she could read it to him.

"It's from Thea," she relayed. "No signs of the shooter. Also, Bo is only seventeen, and he lawyered up."

The first wasn't a surprise, since the shooter was probably long gone by now. But seventeen! That meant Bo was a juvenile and might not be charged as an adult. That could be especially true if Bo didn't have a record. Of course, he had tried to slip a gun into a hospital room, and that was a serious enough charge that he might end up with some actual jail time.

"Text her back," Court instructed, "and ask her to question Bo as soon as his lawyer arrives. I want to find out if he knows who hired Hallie to give him the gun and the drugs."

Bo probably didn't know the answer to that, but they had to try. Right now, Bo was the only living link they had to the dead woman.

Rayna was about to hand him back his phone, but it rang before she could do that. This time it wasn't a number he recognized, and he motioned for Rayna to answer it. She did and put it on speaker. Court braced himself in case this was the shooter, but it wasn't.

It was Raleigh.

"I've got something that I'm sure you'll want to see," Raleigh immediately said. "The coffee shop here doesn't have a security camera, but there's one at the bank across the street. I'm emailing the footage to you now."

That was a pleasant surprise. "Is my mother's meeting with the PI on the footage?" Court asked.

"Yeah. It's grainy because of the glass window that's between them and the camera, but you can see their faces well enough. At first, your mother doesn't appear to be agitated, but that changes at about the five-minute mark. She appears to start crying."

Hell. That could mean that Jennifer had told Helen about the affair. But why would the PI have done that?

"I don't see any exchange of money or anything," Raleigh went on. "And your mother didn't stay long in the coffee shop after that."

So, a short meeting. One that had upset his mother. Coupled with the fact that Helen hadn't mentioned the meeting until he'd asked her about it, it wasn't looking good.

"You'll let me know what your mother has to say about this after you've viewed the footage?" Raleigh asked.

"That might be a while." Court debated how much he should say and then went with the truth. After all, Raleigh would be hearing it soon enough, anyway. "My mother tried to kill herself. Pills. I won't be able to question her until I get the all clear from her doctor."

"Sorry about that." And even though Raleigh had muttered it, he sounded genuine. "We're in a bad place right now with our mothers. Alma hasn't tried to end her life, but she's not as strong as she looks."

"Is she strong enough to have hired a killer?" Court blurted out. He wished though that he'd toned it down a little, since Raleigh actually seemed to want to get to the bottom of this.

"As her son, I'll say no. As a cop, I'll say anyone is capable of pretty much anything. But ask yourself this—if my mother was so upset at Warren, then why would she have waited two months to go after him?"

"Maybe because it took her that long to put a plan together." But Court had to shake his head. "How long ago did my mom meet with the PI?"

"Four days," Raleigh readily answered.

That meant Helen had had that meeting three days before Warren had been shot. If his mother had learned of the affair at the meeting, it was possible she'd somehow gotten Jennifer to help her with a plan. It sickened Court to think that might be true because the plan had included setting up Rayna. Plus, both Rayna and his father could have been killed along with the two women who'd been murdered.

"I'm not saying either of our mothers killed anyone," Raleigh went on, "but we have to consider they could have hired someone who went rogue. Someone they can no longer control."

Yes, and that someone had maybe fired shots at Rayna and him.

Court's phone beeped with an incoming call, and when he saw John Clary's name on the screen, he knew he'd need to talk to his fellow deputy. "I'll review the footage and get back to you," he told Raleigh and switched over the call.

"Please tell me you found the shooter," Court immediately said.

"No. But we do have a problem. Someone tripped the security alarm at Rayna's house. And since it's still taped off as a crime scene, I came here to check it out. There's someone here all right, but he or she ran into the barn when they spotted the cruiser. I just wanted to make sure it wasn't Rayna or someone she sent out here."

"It's not me," Rayna assured him. "But this morning Court had some of his hands go over and tend my horses. Maybe it was one of them."

"Seems funny though that the person would take off running like that," John commented.

It did, and it put an uneasy feeling in Court's stomach. Besides, those hands would have been long finished by now and back at the McCall Ranch.

"Every now and then some kids will come out to my place," Rayna added. "I think I'm the local bogeyman, since many people believe I killed Bobby Joe."

She glanced away from Court when she added that. It was a reminder that her life probably hadn't been so great in the past three years.

"So, you think it might be just a prank or something?" John pressed.

"I don't know," Rayna said after a long pause. "The kids don't usually go in my barn."

None of this was giving Court assurances that all was well. "Are you alone?" he asked John.

"Yeah. I was headed back to the office when I got the call. You think I should get some backup?"

It wasn't an easy question to answer. The sheriff's office was maxed out, and Rayna and he were only a couple of miles from her place. Court turned in that direction, but he definitely wasn't sure it was the right thing to do. He also motioned for the other deputy and Ranger to follow them.

"Just stay put," Court told John. "I'll be there

in a few minutes." He ended the call and immediately looked at Rayna. "You won't be getting out of this cruiser. Understand?"

She didn't argue with that, but she huffed. "You really think the shooter would be stupid enough to go to my house?"

"He might if he thought he'd left something when he attacked you."

That put some new fear back in her eyes, and Court nearly turned around to get Rayna out of there. Then he saw a familiar car on the road just ahead of them.

Whitney.

Rayna immediately took out her phone and tried to call the woman again. Again, it went straight to voice mail.

Court had another decision to make. He wanted to talk to Whitney, but he wasn't sure it was worth putting Rayna at risk this way. That decision was taken out of his hands though when Whitney pulled off onto the shoulder of the road. She got out of her car, and she'd obviously seen them because she started flagging them down.

"Stay inside the cruiser," Court repeated to Rayna. He drew his gun and pulled up behind Whitney. However, he didn't get out, and he only lowered his window a couple of inches.

Dakota stopped his vehicle behind them and did the same thing.

"What are you doing out here?" Court snapped when Whitney ran up to the car.

She practically stopped in her tracks, and she pulled back her shoulders. "What's wrong? What's going on?" She looked at Rayna when she asked that second question.

"You tell us. Why are you here?" he repeated.

She opened her mouth, her attention volleying between Rayna and him. "Mitch. Did he call you, too?"

Mitch? Court certainly hadn't expected her to say that.

"No," Rayna answered, "but I've been trying to call you for the past half hour."

"I know. I'm sorry, but the battery died, and—"

"You didn't tell me you knew one of the dead women," Rayna interrupted.

Whitney shook her head. "I don't."

"You do," Rayna argued. "I saw a picture of you with her. Her name was Jennifer Reeves."

It took several moments for Whitney to process that. Or maybe she was pretending to process it. "The dead woman is Jennifer? I thought her name was Janet."

"She was using an alias," Court explained. "So, you did know her?"

"Of course." Whitney's voice was barely a whisper now, and if she was faking it, she was doing a darn good job. "Jennifer's dead?"

Court verified that with a nod. "When's the last time you saw her?" And that was the first of many questions he had for her.

She shook her head again, pushed her hair from her face. "Months. Maybe longer. We met on a cruise about ten years ago and have stayed in touch." She uttered a hoarse sob. "I can't believe she's dead."

Again, her shock seemed genuine, and later he intended to question her more about her friendship with Jennifer. For now though, there was something more pressing. "What does Mitch have to do with you being out here?"

Whitney paused again as if trying to gather her thoughts. "He called me, and he sounded frantic. Maybe scared. It was a really bad connection with a lot of static, but I thought he said there was something in Rayna's house that he had to get."

"Something?" Court questioned.

Whitney glanced away. "He didn't say exactly what, but I think he maybe meant a gun.

He could be looking for the gun that he thinks killed Bobby Joe."

Both Court and Rayna groaned. "And why did Mitch think the gun would be there after all this time?"

"I don't know. That's about the time my phone battery completely died, and I started driving out here. I was afraid the Rangers would still be here, would see him and think maybe he was the person who'd shot at Rayna and you."

They might have indeed thought that, but it was still no reason for Mitch to run.

"Get in your car and go to the sheriff's office," Court told Whitney.

"But what about Mitch?"

"I'll take care of him."

Whitney didn't look at all comfortable with that. *Well, welcome to the club.* Court wasn't comfortable with it, either, but he didn't want Mitch trespassing on a crime scene, especially with another of their suspects around.

And Whitney was indeed still a suspect.

She'd had explanations as to why she hadn't told them about Jennifer or answered her phone, but Court wanted to do some more digging into her story.

"You want me to take Rayna back to the station with me?" Whitney asked.

"No." Court couldn't answer that fast enough. He raised his window and drove off, leaving Whitney there to gape at them. Probably to curse them, too, since she didn't look very happy with Court's obvious mistrust of her.

Court considered calling John to let him know that Mitch was likely the intruder, but he decided against that, since they were nearly at Rayna's house. Plus, it might not be Mitch at all, and he didn't want John walking into the barn and finding a gunman waiting for him.

"Keep watch around us," Court reminded Rayna, though he was certain she was already doing that. They were both on edge.

When her house finally came into view, he had no trouble seeing that the front door was wide-open. He also spotted John. The deputy had taken cover behind his cruiser and had his gun drawn. And Court soon realized why.

Mitch had his hands raised in the air, and he was coming out of the barn. "Don't shoot," Mitch called out to them.

Court parked next to John so that the deputy's cruiser would also be between Rayna and

Mitch, and he took aim. Behind him, Dakota and the Texas Ranger did the same thing.

"Mitch, are you armed?" Court asked.

Mitch tipped his head to the barn. "I was, but I left it in there. Didn't want either of you getting trigger-happy when you saw me trying to do your jobs."

Court didn't like the sound of that, but then he rarely liked anything Mitch said. "And doing our job includes trespassing on private property and breaking and entering?" Court fired back.

"Yes, in this case. I didn't get a chance to try the security code or the key. The door was busted open when I got here."

That didn't make sense, and Court was about to demand more, but Mitch looked past John and Court and into the cruiser where Rayna was sitting.

"You might not have actually murdered my brother, but you're not off the hook," Mitch said to her, and he smiled.

That brought Rayna out of the cruiser. "What are you talking about?" It was the exact question Court had been about to ask.

"Are you admitting Rayna didn't kill Bobby Joe?" Court demanded.

Mitch nodded.

That nod might have been a simple gesture, but Court could hear the sound it caused Rayna to make. She gasped. "He's alive," she muttered.

Mitch nodded again, and he stopped when he was about ten feet from them. "I need to get my phone from my pocket, and I don't want you to shoot me when I do that." He waited until Court nodded before Mitch took out his cell. "Bobby Joe left me a message. That's why I called Whitney and told her to come. She'll want to hear this, too."

"She can hear it later," Court snapped.

Mitch nodded, pressed the play button, and he held the cell up in the air for them to hear. It didn't take long before Court heard the voice.

"It's Bobby Joe. Meet me at Rayna's."

There was a lot of static, and the message was choppy as if he'd been thinking about each word before he said it.

"The security code is seven-six-two-one," the message continued, "and there's a spare key in the birdhouse on the end of the porch." The static got even worse. "I want to show you where she hid the gun. The gun she used to try to kill me."

Chapter Eleven

The message kept repeating through Rayna's head, and she couldn't make it stop. Bobby Joe was alive.

But now he was accusing her of attempted murder.

She'd denied it the moment she'd heard the message, and she thought Court believed her. Not Mitch though. But then, he'd always thought the worst of her. And would continue to think it, too, now that Mitch had heard the accusation from his own brother.

"There is no smoking gun," she said to Court. "So why would Bobby Joe tell Mitch to meet me at his house?"

"Maybe to plant something to incriminate you," Court said without hesitating. Which meant that message was likely replaying in his head, as well.

Not necessarily a good thing, since they

were both trying to focus on the drive back to the sheriff's office. Dakota hadn't followed them for this part of the trip. That was because Court had wanted the Ranger to go ahead and take Mitch to the sheriff's office so that Dakota could stay behind and search for Bobby Joe. Rayna had wanted to do that, too, but it wouldn't have been very smart, since Bobby Joe could have just gunned her down. Of course, maybe he wanted to torment her first, to punish her for breaking off things with him.

"Everyone knows now that you didn't kill him," Court said. "I'm sorry for not believing you in the first place."

"There was a lot of circumstantial evidence," she reminded him. Evidence that Bobby Joe had planted. "He must have stockpiled some of his own blood that he put in my kitchen."

Court made a sound of agreement. "And he made sure he cleaned it up in such a way to make us believe you'd tried to cover up the crime scene." He stopped, cursed. "It could have worked, too. You could be in jail right now."

Since it was obvious he was beating himself up about that, Rayna touched his arm. "It's okay. Right now, I'm more concerned about what Bobby Joe's going to do next."

"He'll try to kill you," Court quickly answered. "That's why you'll need to stay in protective custody. That's why we have to find him. We might get lucky and be able to trace his call to Mitch."

Yes, and that brought her back to the message Bobby Joe had left on Mitch's phone. Why risk bringing in anyone else, even his brother? Why not just plant the gun and then arrange for someone to find it? And why do the whole gun-planting thing if Bobby Joe was the one behind the attacks? Why not just continue the attacks until he was successful?

A thought that twisted her stomach into a knot.

But there was something else about this that didn't fit.

"The security code," Rayna said. "The one Bobby Joe gave Mitch. It was the old code. That's why he tripped the security alarm when he tried to get in."

"Did you know about the key in the birdhouse?" Court asked.

"No, but if he was telling the truth about that, it would have been the old one, too. I changed the locks after the trial."

And Court obviously picked up on where she was leading with this because he cursed.

"It means Bobby Joe wasn't the person who broke into your house and drugged you."

No, because whoever had done that had the correct key and code. With everything else going on, she hadn't followed up on finding who could have gotten those things, but she had to move that to the front burner.

Well, as soon as she dealt with the news of Bobby Joe's return.

Even though she'd known he was alive, it was another thing to deal with the proof of it. Plus, he was out there, probably trying to figure out his next move. He probably hadn't counted on that move including Mitch ratting him out.

They pulled to a stop in front of the sheriff's office, and Rayna immediately saw the cruiser the Ranger had used to bring back Mitch. What was missing was Whitney's car, but Rayna held out hope that her friend had parked elsewhere and walked to the station. She didn't want to accept just yet that Whitney could be avoiding her because she'd had something to do with those attacks.

"The Ranger had to leave and go back to the hospital to guard your dad, but Ian just went in the interview room with Mitch to take his statement," Thea said the moment Court and

Rayna walked in. "Is it true? Is Bobby Joe really alive?"

"It's true," Court verified.

But he didn't stop to add more. With his arm hooked around Rayna's waist, he kept her moving to Egan's office, where he had her sit in a chair next to the desk. He also shut the door.

He stared at her as if waiting for something, and that was when Rayna realized he was looking at her hands. They were shaking. Heck, she was shaking. And before she even knew it was going to happen, the tears came.

The emotions hit her all at once. For three years she'd been battling the stigma of being branded a killer, and that wasn't just going away despite the fact of Bobby Joe's return. She'd hated him for a long time now but never so much as in this moment. Bobby Joe had taken her life and torn it into little pieces, and he was still tearing it, still trying to break her.

"I don't want to cry," she insisted. But that didn't stop the tears.

Court grabbed her some tissues, but instead of just handing them to her, he wiped her face. Their eyes met. And she saw more of that frustration and guilt in his expression. Yes, she could see that even through the tears.

He muttered some profanity, pulled her to

her feet and eased her into his arms. "You can yell at me if it'll make you feel better."

She didn't want to yell at anyone. Especially Court. Right now, he was the only sane thing in her life.

That stopped her.

And Rayna felt herself go stiff. Court obviously felt it, too, because he looked down at her. Again, he seemed to be waiting for something, but she didn't know what exactly.

Not until he kissed her, that was.

Even though she figured he was doing this to comfort her, Rayna instantly got a jolt of other emotions. Familiar ones. Because the kiss spurred the old fires between them. And it kept on stirring it because he continued to kiss her. This went well past the comforting stage, especially when he pulled her against him.

Court made a sound, a grumble from deep within his chest. It seemed like some kind of protest, maybe a plea for him to stop. But he didn't. He continued the kiss until the taste of him was sliding right through her.

Yes, this was a cure for tears, but it soon gave her a new problem. The touch of his chest against her breasts, the way he took her mouth... that only made her want him even more.

Rayna found herself slipping her arms around his neck to bring him even closer. Not that she could actually do that. Not while they were clothed anyway, and there was little chance of them stripping down in Egan's office. However, there was still a chance of things escalating.

Court backed her against the door, and the kiss raged on. Until they were out of breath. Until Rayna was certain she could take no more. Only then did he pull back from her, and she braced herself. Court would almost certainly curse and remind her that kissing her had been a huge mistake.

He didn't.

But she saw something else in his eyes that she hadn't wanted to see. Sympathy. He was feeling sorry for her, maybe because he and his father hadn't believed her about Bobby Joe. Maybe because he knew she was probably very close to losing it. Either way, she didn't want that from him, and that was why she moved to the side.

"We should review the security footage Raleigh emailed to you," she managed to say. Not easily. It was hard to talk with her breath thin and her head light. “And talk to Mitch. Plus, Whitney will be here soon.”

She would have gone back into the squad room to his desk if Court hadn’t caught her hand. He looked at her as if trying to figure out what was going on in her head. Then he cursed.

“That wasn’t a pity kiss,” he snarled. “Trust me, when I kiss, it’s for just one reason, and it doesn’t have anything to do with pity.”

That pretty much took care of what little breath she had, but he didn’t give her a chance to respond. He threw open the door and went to his desk.

Thea glanced up from her computer screen but then quickly looked away. She could no doubt see what was going on between them and had wisely decided to stay out of it.

“Any updates on my father?” Court asked Thea. He sat at his desk and started downloading the email from Raleigh.

“Nothing, but I’m hoping in this case that no news is good news.”

Rayna agreed. “What about Whitney? Have you seen her? She was supposed to come in.”

That was definitely a surprise to Thea. “No sign of her. Should I call her?”

"No," Court answered. "I'll deal with Whitney, but I am going to need you to run that trace on the phone call he got from his brother. Did Mitch ask for a lawyer before Ian went in to take his statement?"

"No. I suspect he will though if he really did break into Rayna's house."

"He claims someone else did the actual breaking in," Court said. "What about Bo's lawyer?"

"Not here yet, either. He called and said he was stuck in San Antonio, so it might be a couple more hours."

Rayna wished they could get the answers from the teenager now, but it was possible that Bo was going to be a dead end when it came to helping them with this investigation.

While Thea got to work on the phone trace, Court loaded the security footage. "Raleigh said my mom's demeanor changed at the five-minute mark, but I want to watch it from the start."

He pulled up a chair for her, their gazes connecting again when she sat. "For the record, I didn't let you kiss me out of pity," she whispered.

The corner of his mouth lifted for just a second, but that seemed to indicate they'd declared some kind of truce. Rayna was okay with that, especially since the images loaded on the screen, and she knew that had to push kissing, and thoughts of kissing, to the side. That didn't mean this heat was going away though.

Rayna leaned in closer to the monitor when she spotted Helen making her way to the coffee shop. She certainly didn't look upset.

As Raleigh had warned them, the images weren't so clear when Helen went inside, but they could still see when she greeted Jennifer with a handshake. After that, the women sat at a table so that only the sides of their bodies were facing the camera.

"Too bad this doesn't have sound," Court mumbled as they reached the five-minute mark.

Rayna agreed because there was definitely a difference in Helen's body language. "Maybe your mom was just upset about reliving the details of Hannah's murder."

"Maybe." But he didn't sound especially hopeful about that.

They watched as Alma came in through the other entrance, and as the woman had said, she stayed back behind a half wall that would have hidden her from view of Helen and Jennifer.

Alma hadn't been in the shop very long when Helen stood. She took something that Jennifer handed her, perhaps a business card, and slipped it into her purse before she hurried out.

Once Helen was outside, it was easier to see her face. She wiped at her eyes as if wiping away tears and then disappeared out of camera range. Court reached to turn off the footage but then stopped.

They both zoomed in on the man who was outside of the coffee shop. He was in position to have watched the meeting between Helen and Jennifer, and now he was watching Helen as she left. And the man was someone they both recognized.

Mitch.

"Mitch sure as hell didn't mention any of this," Court grumbled, and he got to his feet. "I think it's time to question him."

"So do I, but why would he have been spying on them? You think Jennifer told him about the meeting?"

"That's my guess. I'm betting Mitch knows a lot more about Jennifer than he's letting on." He started for the door but then stopped when Rayna's phone rang. "If that's Whitney, tell her to get her butt in here right now."

But it wasn't Whitney's name on the screen.

It was Unknown Caller.

She hadn't thought her stomach could tighten even more, but it did. Rayna showed the screen to Court and waited until he got out his own phone to record the conversation before she answered the call and put it on speaker.

Nothing. Not for several long moments.

"Hey, Rayna. It's me," the caller said.

Bobby Joe.

Like the message he'd left for Mitch, this one was filled with static, too.

"Can't wait to see you," Bobby Joe added.

Rayna could have sworn her heart went to her knees, and she fired glances outside the window. There was a trickle of people on the sidewalks, but there was no sign of Bobby Joe.

"Where are you?" Court snapped.

There was a long pause. "Rayna's gonna pay for what she did."

Rayna hated that he could still get to her like this, and she mustered up as much steel as she could manage. "Is that a threat?"

Bobby Joe didn't confirm that, but after another hesitation, he just laughed.

It did indeed feel like a threat. And there was nothing she could do about it. Not unless they caught Bobby Joe, that was. Then he could be charged with fraud for trying to frame her for his murder.

"Bye, Rayna," Bobby Joe added. "See you soon." And the call ended.

Chapter Twelve

Court could feel the dangerous energy bubbling up inside him, and he hated what this was doing to Rayna. All those feelings and energy were so strong that they almost overshadowed his lawman's instincts.

"Something's not right," he said.

That caused Rayna to fire glances all around them again.

"No, I don't think Bobby Joe is nearby," Court added. "In fact, I'm not sure that call was actually from him. I think it was a recording of old conversations that have been spliced together."

She opened her mouth as if she might dispute that, but then Rayna frowned. She was obviously going back through what she'd heard. "Maybe."

"That would account for the static and the long pauses in between some of the words."

Rayna shook her head. "But who would do that? Why would someone want to make us believe it was Bobby Joe?"

"Maybe to rattle us." And if so, that had worked. But Court got the feeling there was much more to it than that.

He handed his phone to Thea. "I recorded a call that Bobby Joe supposedly just made. I need the voice analyzed on it. Also the voice on the message left for Mitch."

Thea nodded. "I've already started working on tracing that call to Mitch. It came from a burner, so no luck."

That was too bad. A burner was a prepaid cell phone that couldn't be traced.

"But I did find something strange," Thea added a moment later. "Using that same burner, someone called Mitch three times before leaving that message. It appears Mitch answered the other three calls, but Bobby Joe or whoever it was didn't talk to him. Or if he did, they were very short conversations. It appears the only time the caller actually communicated was through the message he left on the fourth call that Mitch didn't answer."

Yeah, that was strange, and it was right in line with Court's theory about Bobby Joe's conversation being spliced together. Maybe someone had taken old recordings and used them.

But again. Court didn't know why.

"I'm done with his phone," Thea added. "I've gotten everything I can from it—including copying the message from Bobby Joe. Now I'm just waiting on the phone company to email a complete record of all the calls and texts he's made in the past couple of months."

It might take a while to get that, especially since Mitch wasn't being charged with a serious crime.

"I can give Mitch back his phone when I talk to him," Court said, taking it from her.

Thea nodded again. "It can't wait until Ian is done taking his statement?" she asked. Her concern wasn't because she had doubts about his interrogation skills. It was because Mitch was a hothead who could set off Court's own temper.

"No. I'm not going to interview him right now. I just want to ask him about that message."

Thea still looked a little skeptical. So did Rayna, and she followed him to the interview room. Ian was typing something on a laptop. It was no doubt Mitch's statement.

Mitch immediately got to his feet when Court opened the door. "Did they find Bobby Joe?"

Court shook his head and quietly apologized to Ian for interrupting the interview.

"You're sure your brother is actually alive?" Court asked Mitch. He put the man's phone on the table next to him.

The surprise went through Mitch's eyes. "Of course he is. You heard the message."

"I heard what could have been something recorded years ago. Something that was put together to make you believe it was actually from Bobby Joe."

"It was from him," Mitch practically shouted. But then he stopped and slid glances at both of them. "Is this some kind of trick?"

"You tell me," Court argued.

"If you're accusing me of...whatever the hell this is, then I want a lawyer." Mitch's voice got even louder, and his hands went to his hips. "And I want bail. You can't lock me up for trespassing."

Well, he could put him in jail, but Court couldn't hold him for long, since right now the only charge he could make against Mitch was a misdemeanor. But maybe there was another way of going about this.

"Can you think of a reason why someone would want you to fake that message?" Court asked.

"No! My brother wanted to meet me. He

wanted to show me the gun that Rayna has hidden somewhere."

Not likely. There'd been plenty of searches of Rayna's place that should have already revealed a gun if there was one. Of course, Bobby Joe could have hidden it as he'd maybe done when he'd put the key in the birdhouse.

And that led Court to an idea.

Bobby Joe might not try to see Mitch as long as he was here, but if he was indeed alive, he might contact Mitch as soon as no cops were around.

"You'll be able to leave as soon as you're done with the interview," Court told Mitch.

Ian made eye contact with Court and seemed to know what Court was thinking. "We're done. Well, unless you're going to press charges against him for trespassing," Ian said to Rayna.

She glanced at all of them. Paused. Then shook her head. "No charges unless we prove Mitch actually broke down the door."

"I didn't," Mitch insisted.

Maybe he was telling the truth, but it didn't matter. "Just stop by Thea's desk," Court told Mitch. "She'll print out a copy of what Ian just typed up so you can read through it and sign it. Will you need a ride?"

"Thanks, but no, thanks. I left my truck on a trail near Rayna's, but I'll find a way to get home." Mitch grabbed his phone and hurried out of the room.

"I know it's a risk, letting him walk," Court said to Rayna.

"But it might help us catch Bobby Joe," she finished for him. "If he's really alive, that is."

Yes, that was the million-dollar question, but Mitch might be able to give them the answer to that.

"You want me to follow him?" Ian asked the moment that Mitch was out of earshot.

Court nodded. "But I don't want you to go alone. And we don't have another available deputy." He didn't like this much, but it was a temporary solution until he could get some Rangers in place to pick up the tail on Mitch. "Rayna and I will go with you."

Ian didn't look so certain about that. Neither was Court, but he had no intentions of leaving her at the sheriff's office, where Thea already had her hands full.

"It'll be okay," he told Rayna. Without thinking, he brushed a kiss on her cheek.

He immediately cursed himself for doing that. Yeah, that other kiss had definitely broken down some barriers that should have stayed in place. At least until this investigation was over.

Court texted Thea to let her know what was going on, and Ian, Rayna and he went out the back to one of the two unmarked cars they kept there. It was reinforced just like a cruiser, but maybe Mitch wouldn't recognize it was a cop car. Ian got behind the wheel, and after Court got in the back seat with Rayna, Ian pulled to the side of the building so they'd be able to see when Mitch left.

Court was so caught up in keeping watch that it gave him a jolt when the sound of his phone ringing shot through the car. Not Unknown Caller this time. It was Rachel.

"How's Mom?" he asked the moment he answered.

"Not great. They're transferring her to the hospital in San Antonio." Rachel was crying. No doubt about that. Court could hear her sobs. "They'll commit her there until she can have some evals done."

"You need me there?" Though he wasn't sure how he would manage it. Still, he would if necessary.

"No need. We won't be here much longer, and Mom won't be allowed visitors for a while at the other hospital."

That meant Court wouldn't be able to question his mother anytime soon about what he'd seen on the surveillance footage. However, there might be a way around that. "By any chance did Mom bring her purse to the hospital?"

He could tell from Rachel's slight huff that the question had surprised her. "No. It's at the house. Why?"

Court hoped he didn't alarm Rachel unnecessarily with this, but it was something they had to know. "I believe she might have gotten a business card or something from the murdered PI, Jennifer Reeves. That was a couple of days ago. I know it's a long shot, but I need to see if she still has it."

Rachel's slight gasp let him know that he'd alarmed her after all. "I'll be going back to the ranch when Mom is transferred. I want to get some things and go to the hospital in San Antonio. I can check her purse as soon as I'm back at the house."

"Thanks. But I don't want you driving alone."

"Egan's already told me that. He'll take me back, and then we'll drive to San Antonio together. He's arranging to have some local cops guard me."

Good. He thanked her again and ended the call when he saw Mitch finally come out of the building. The man didn't even look their way. He immediately took out his phone, made a call and started walking on the sidewalk away from them. Ian eased out of the parking lot so they could follow him.

Mitch had made it only about a block when Court's phone rang again. For a moment he thought it was Mitch calling him, but it was Whitney's name on the screen. Court pressed the answer button, ready to blast her for not coming directly to the sheriff's office as he'd ordered her to do. However, Whitney spoke before Court could say anything.

"Oh, God. You've got to help me!" Whitney blurted out. "Oh, God. There's a fire."

And then Court heard something on the other end of the line that he definitely didn't want to hear.

The sound of a gunshot.

RAYNA HAD NO trouble hearing the sound. Or Whitney's bone-chilling scream that quickly followed the blast from what had to be a gunshot.

"Whitney?" Court yelled into the phone. "Where are you? What's going on?"

"You have to help me," Whitney begged. "I'm just up the street by the hardware store."

That was the direction Mitch was walking. The direction that Ian went as well, and both Court and he drew their guns.

The hardware store was about two blocks away, but the moment Ian pulled out of the parking lot, Rayna saw the smoke. It was thick and black, billowing in the air, and the wind was blowing it right toward them.

Mitch obviously noticed it, too, because he turned and started running back to the sheriff's office. Maybe he would stay there instead of trying to get to Bobby Joe. That way, someone could still follow him after they took care of this situation.

"I'm calling the fire department," Ian said, and he did that while he continued to drive closer to the smoke. It wouldn't take the fire department long to get there at all. Well, it wouldn't take long if there wasn't any other gunfire.

"Get down on the seat," Court told her, and he handed her his phone. "Try to find out exactly where Whitney is and who fired that shot."

Rayna did get down, and she tried to level her voice. Whitney had sounded terrified, and it wouldn't do the woman any good if she heard the panic in Rayna's tone, too.

"Where are you?" Rayna asked.

Whitney started coughing, which meant she was probably very close to the smoke. Maybe in the middle of it. "I think I saw Bobby Joe."

So, not just a message or phone call this time but a possible sighting. Of course, Hallie had posed as Rayna, so someone could be doing the same when it came to Bobby Joe. "Where did you see him?"

"In the alley by the hardware store." Whitney coughed some more. "I'm not sure he saw me, so I went running after him. I saw a car parked back there, but that's when the fire started. The flames just popped up right in front of me, and I couldn't get to him."

Which meant someone had almost certainly set it. Before Rayna could ask her who'd fired the shot, there was another one. Then another. They sounded much too close, which was probably why Ian pulled off the street and into a parking place outside the bookstore.

"Everyone, take cover now!" Court shouted when he lowered his window.

Rayna could hear people running and shouting. She prayed that none of them would be hurt.

"Where are you?" Whitney said on another of those sobs. "I need to find you. And we need to find Bobby Joe so he can clear your name once and for all."

"No. You need to go inside the nearest building and stay put," Rayna assured her. "You could be shot."

Whitney said something that she didn't catch, and the line went dead. Rayna didn't try to call her back because she didn't want the sound of a ringing phone to cause a gunman to home in on Whitney. Maybe she had done as Rayna told her and had taken cover.

Behind them, she heard the wail of the sirens from the fire engine. But she also heard a fourth shot. It was even closer than the others had been.

The fifth one slammed into the front windshield.

Both deputies cursed, and Court pushed her even farther down on the seat. "You see the shooter?" Ian asked.

"No." But Court was glancing all around them. "Tell the fire department not to approach. It's too dangerous."

Another shot cracked through the air, and this one hit just a few inches from the previous one. The glass held, but it was cracked enough that other bullets might be able to get through.

"Get us out of here," Court told Ian.

The deputy did. The moment he finished with radioing the fire department, Ian threw the car into Reverse and hit the gas. He didn't get far though, probably because of other vehicles.

"Hold on," Ian told them.

His warning came only a few seconds before he made a sharp turn, causing Court and Rayna to slam against each other. She lifted her head enough to see that Ian had turned around in the middle of the street and was now heading back in the direction of the sheriff's office.

The shooter fired a flurry of shots at the car, all slamming into the back windshield.

"I see the guy," Court said.

She followed his gaze to the left side of the street. The same side as the fire. But she was too far down on the seat to see what had captured his attention.

"It's a man wearing a mask," Court added.

It was probably the same person who'd shot at them at the hospital. But had he also been the one to set the fire? And if so, why? Maybe he thought it would conceal him, and if so, it'd worked. The guy had managed to get off at least ten shots before Court had spotted him.

"You want me to go back?" Ian asked.

She saw the quick debate in Court's eyes. He wanted to catch this guy and would have almost certainly gone after him if she hadn't been in the car. "No. Let's take Rayna to the sheriff's office. We'll regroup and go after him."

Which meant Court was going to put himself in the line of fire. Of course, that was his job, but it sickened her to think that he could be hurt or worse because some goon was after her.

Ian screeched to a stop in front of the sheriff's office, but none of them got out. They sat there, no doubt waiting to see if the shooter would continue. If he did, it wasn't safe for them to run inside. Even though they would be out in the open only a couple of seconds, that would be enough time for them to be gunned down.

Rayna lifted her head again. Thea was in the doorway of the sheriff's office, and she had her gun drawn. There was no sign of Mitch, but Court's phone rang again, and she saw Whitney's name on the screen. Rayna answered it as fast as she could.

"Please tell me you took cover," Rayna told her.

"I couldn't. For your sake, I had to find Bobby Joe."

Rayna groaned. "No, you don't. There's a gunman out there."

"Yes. I saw him. Are you sure it was a man? I thought maybe it was a woman wearing a ski mask."

That gave Rayna a jolt of adrcnaline. It wouldn't be Court's mom, since she was on her way to a hospital in San Antonio, but it could be Alma. Still, that seemed like a stretch. If Alma wanted them dead, she could have just hired someone. That included a female assassin.

Whitney gasped, the sound coming through loud and clear. "Rayna, tell Court he needs to get here. He needs to see this."

That didn't help with the adrenaline, either. "See what?" Rayna pressed.

"Oh, God. There's a body in that fire."

Chapter Thirteen

Court didn't like anything about this, but there wasn't much else he could do but stand and watch as the fire department finished up with what was now a crime scene.

One with a body.

Once they were done, the medical examiner and CSIs could get in the alley and maybe figure out what had gone on here. He could question not only the fire chief, Delbert Monroe, but also help track down possible witnesses. Until that happened, Court could only speculate. And worry about Rayna.

He'd left her at the sheriff's office with Thea and Ian, and Egan was on the way now that he'd put the ranch on lockdown. Three lawmen would hopefully be enough to keep her safe, but she was in the building with not only Bo but Whitney, as well. At least Bo was still locked up, but he couldn't do the same to Whitney because there were no charges against her. Still, that didn't mean Court trusted her.

Ditto for Mitch.

But Court hadn't heard a peep from the man since he'd left shortly before the fire. He wasn't answering his phone, and no one had seen him. That meant Mitch could have been the person who'd worn a ski mask and shot at them. He would have had time to duck into the alley and do that.

Whitney had said though that she thought the shooter was a woman. So far, no other witness had managed to corroborate that, but it didn't mean she was mistaken or lying. That was because their other suspect—Alma—wasn't answering her phone, either.

No, there wasn't any part of this he liked.

Plus, there was the whole problem of an unidentified shooter. There hadn't been any shots fired in over an hour, so that probably meant the gunman was long gone. That didn't mean he wouldn't be back though.

Court took out his phone to call and check on Rayna, but he finally saw Delbert making his way toward him. He was sporting a weary expression, along with soot and ashes on his clothes.

"Our DB is male," Delbert said right off the

bat. "We didn't touch the body, of course, but it's badly burned. Too burned to make a visual ID."

That didn't surprise Court because the vehicle that had contained the body was a charred mess. "I smell gasoline," Court pointed out.

Delbert nodded. "An accelerant was used. I suspect it was poured over the car and then lit. Most of his clothes burned off, but there's some tissue remaining. Plus, his teeth are in good shape. We can compare them to dental records."

Good. Because the person's identity might lead Court to finding out why he was dead. "Any signs that the guy struggled to get out of the burning car?"

"No. He was lying on the back seat."

That possibly meant he was unconscious or even already dead before the fire. Often criminals tried to use fire to cover up any DNA or trace evidence they might have left behind. Of course, it would be bold for a criminal to do that in broad daylight.

Or maybe not bold after all.

Court motioned to the blackened strip on the concrete between the dead guy's car and them. It was where a second fire had been set, and it was a good fifteen feet from the other deadly one. “Can you think of any good reason why someone would do that?”

Delbert immediately shook his head. “No, but I can think of a bad one. A strip fire like that would conceal whatever was going on in the car.”

Yeah, that’d been Court’s theory, too. If the person who’d set it had been behind the first set of flames, it would have made it very hard for someone on the street to see him or her. Then the person could have escaped through the back alley.

There were no cameras back there, either.

“I went ahead and called in the CSIs,” Delbert went on. “They’ll be here soon.” He hitched his thumb back to the alley. “Just thought you should know there’s a cell phone on the ground. It’s not a fancy smart one. Just one of the cheap ones you can buy just about anywhere. Again, we didn’t touch it, and it might not even belong to the vic.”

Court would definitely have it collected and tested. If it was the vic’s though, he wasn’t sure why it was out of the car when the body was inside.

Delbert glanced around the street, which was empty now. But Delbert wasn’t looking at the sidewalks. He was studying the buildings and the streetlight that was to their right.

"There aren't any cameras," Court told him.

Of course, Court would check to see if anyone had recently added one, but this area of Main Street was essentially a dead zone when it came to surveillance. Alma might not have known that, but Whitney and Mitch likely would have.

Ditto for his mother.

That was because it'd come up in a discussion when there'd been a robbery at the hardware store a couple of years ago. Many people then had lobbied to get security cameras for all of Main Street, but it hadn't been in the budget.

Court wanted to exclude his mother as a suspect, but he kept going back to the point that Raleigh had made. Whoever had hired the shooter might no longer have a leash on him or her. If that proved to be true, then his mom was still a possible person of interest.

When Court saw the CSI van pull up, he figured it was time for him to go back to the station. He could do a lot more good there—including keep watch on Rayna—while the CSIs processed the crime scene. However, he did remind both the CSIs and Delbert to call him the moment they had anything on the body or the phone. Too bad Court couldn't just take it now, but he couldn't touch it until the CSIs had gotten pictures.

Court drove his cruiser back to the sheriff's office, parking behind the shot-up unmarked car. Just seeing it made him feel sick and riled him to the core. Once again, Rayna had come close to being killed, and they still didn't know why.

"Anything?" Rayna asked the moment he stepped inside. She was in the doorway of Egan's office, her hands bracketed on the jamb. Her knuckles were white.

"We'll know something soon," he assured her and hoped that wasn't a lie.

Rayna wasn't alone. Both Thea and Ian were in the squad room, but there was no sign of Whitney.

"Egan got here about fifteen minutes ago, and Whitney's in the interview room with him," Rayna said. "She seemed really upset." Court didn't miss the *seemed*, and he wondered if that meant Rayna was having doubts about her friend.

Because he thought they could both use it, he went to Rayna and pulled her into his arms for a hug. Yeah, he needed it all right, and that was why Court lingered a moment before he eased back from her—along with easing her deeper into Egan's office. Not so he could kiss her, though that was something he suddenly wanted to do. No, it was because the shooter was still at large and could try to fire through the windows of the sheriff's office.

"Did Whitney say anything to you before Egan got here?" Court asked her.

"Not really. She was crying a lot. I asked her why she didn't come straight to the sheriff's office after you told her to, and she said she had to pick up some meds first. She'd felt a migraine coming on."

Since Whitney did indeed suffer from migraines, it wasn't much of a stretch that she'd need meds for the headaches. Still, the timing was suspicious.

"Come on." Court took Rayna by the hand. "We'll go to the observation room and listen to what she's saying to Egan." That was better than standing there with all this energy still zinging between them. "I'll also try again to track down Mitch."

He took out his phone, but it rang before he could make the call. However, this one could be important, since it was from one of the CSIs, Larry Hanson. Court put the call on speaker and hoped it wasn't bad news. They'd already had enough of that for the day.

"I went ahead and photographed the phone," Larry said right off. "I was about to bag it when I saw there was a missed call on the screen. I don't have the password to see if there's a voice mail, but I got the name of the caller."

"Who?" Court immediately asked.

"Alma Lawton. You know her?"

Hell. "Yeah. I know her." And he was going to get her right back in here for questioning. "I don't suppose you can tell whose phone that is?"

"Nope. Not without the password. I'll get it to the lab though to see if they can come up with something. We might have something on the body soon, too."

That got Court's attention. "Dental records?"

"We'll try those, sure, but it seems as if the back of the body might still be intact. The ME thinks he can see a wallet in the back of the guy's jeans. We won't know though until we can lift it, but that shouldn't be much longer."

If there was a wallet, there might be an ID. Of course, it didn't mean the ID or, for that matter, the wallet belonged to the dead guy. However, it could be a good break if it did.

Court thanked Larry and went back into the

squad room so he could get Alma's number from the computer.

"It must not be Alma's phone they found, since she was the caller," Rayna said. "But I don't think she knows any of our other suspects. Not personally, anyway," she added.

Rayna was no doubt referring to his mother. Alma had definitely heard of her, but neither Alma nor Helen had mentioned being in contact with each other.

The moment he had Alma's number, he tried to call her. It went straight to voice mail, so Court left a message for her to get to the sheriff's office ASAP for questioning. He tried Raleigh next, but the deputy who answered said the sheriff was in the process of arresting a burglary suspect. Since Court had struck out with both Alma and Raleigh, he made another call to his sister. Unlike the other two, Rachel answered on the first ring.

"Are you okay?" Rachel asked before he could even say anything.

"We're fine. You?"

"I'm as well as can be expected. Egan said there was a body, that that's why he had to go in."

"There is. The CSIs are working on the ID

right now." He gathered his breath for the next question. "By any chance, did Mom have a new phone? Not the one we got her for Christmas but a cheaper one?"

"I don't think so. But I can look in her purse. I was going to do that anyway because you said you wanted me to check for a business card."

"Yes. Could you do that now?"

Since Rachel was the daughter and sister of lawmen, she knew that wasn't a casual question and that it likely had something to do with the investigation. "What's this all about?"

"Just checking to see if she called anyone."

It was a pretty sorry explanation, and Rachel made a sound to indicate she wasn't buying it. Still, she was obviously looking because several moments later she added, "Her phone's not on her nightstand." Court could hear her moving around. "I'm looking through her purse now. No phone. You think she lost it?"

He hoped not, and he hoped even more that she hadn't bought another phone and used it to call Alma. Of course, even if she had, that wouldn't have explained why it would be in that alley.

"There's a card," Rachel added. "Yes, it's

for Stigler Investigations. You think Jennifer Reeves works for this PI agency?"

No, that hadn't come up at any point, so he sandwiched his phone between his shoulder and ear, went to his desk and typed in the name on his computer. It was another agency all right.

One that specialized in getting proof of cheating spouses.

That felt like a punch to the gut. Because it meant that his mother had likely known about Warren's affair days ago. That would have been plenty enough time to hire someone to fire that shot that'd gone into his father's chest.

"Do you have access to Mom and Dad's bank account?" Court asked.

"No," Rachel answered, hesitation in her voice. "But I'm sure I can get it. Why?"

Court didn't go with the full truth on this. "I just want to see if maybe Mom hired a PI, too. It might have gone on her credit card if she hired someone over the phone. Also, look for a check."

"Now, are you going to tell me what this is all about?" Rachel demanded.

"Just making sure there's not another PI out there to interfere with this investigation." But what he really wanted to know was if there was enough money missing for his mother to have hired a gunman. "Call me if you find anything." With more of that skepticism in her tone, Rachel assured him that she would.

Since it might take a while for Rachel to do that, Court led Rayna to the observation room. Egan and Whitney were there, and Whitney was still crying. He wanted to give her the benefit of the doubt, not only because she was Rayna's friend but also because she worked at the sheriff's office. He hated the possibility that he'd been working with a would-be killer after all these years.

Rayna stared at her friend through the glass. "Whitney hasn't been the same person since my trial. She's been, well, distant."

Maybe because Whitney had thought Rayna was really a killer. But there was another angle on this. "You think Whitney could have had feelings for Bobby Joe?"

"It's possible." Since Rayna hadn't hesitated, it meant she'd given that some thought. Then she shrugged. "But there were times when I felt as if Whitney wanted me to ditch him. Whenever we'd have a girls' night out, she was always trying to fix me up with other guys."

Again, that was maybe because Whitney wanted Bobby Joe for herself. She did seem to be genuinely upset, and maybe that was because of the possible Bobby Joe sighting.

"Who do you think set the fire?" Egan asked her.

Whitney's head whipped up. "You're not accusing me of doing that, are you?" There was some bitterness in her voice.

"Just asking," Egan calmly clarified.

"Well, I don't know. I told you the flames just shot up right in front of me. I would have caught up with Bobby Joe if it hadn't been for that."

If she was telling the truth, it meant someone had put that line of gasoline there before Whitney had even gone into the alley, and it was possible someone had triggered it with a remote device.

But why?

That was the question Court was asking himself when his phone rang, and he saw Larry's name on the screen.

"We got the wallet from our dead guy," Larry immediately said. "And there was a driver's license. The name on it is Dustin Clark, but the photo is one I'm sure you'll recognize. I'm texting it to you now."

Court knew Larry was right the moment he loaded the photo and saw the man's face.

Bobby Joe.

HE WAS FINALLY DEAD.

For the first time in three years, Rayna actually believed that was true—that Bobby Joe was no longer a threat to her. Of course, they'd have to wait for more proof of the dental records, but she didn't need anything else.

"You should sit down," she heard Court say.

He didn't wait for her to do that though. He practically put her in the chair in the observation room. That was when Rayna realized she was wobbling some and wasn't feeling very steady. Court probably thought she was about to collapse. She was, but it was from relief.

That relief didn't last long though.

"Will people once again think I killed Bobby Joe?" she asked.

Court shook his head, sighed and brushed a kiss on the top of her head. All of those gestures eased some of the gut-wrenching tension inside her. "You were with Ian and me when that fire started."

True, but since many people in McCall Canyon thought she was a killer, they might think she'd set this up in some way.

"Who would have killed him?" Rayna pressed.

Court shrugged. "For us to know that, we'll have to figure out what he's been doing all this time. I doubt this was suicide, so that means either someone killed him in the car and set fire to it or they put him in the vehicle after he was already dead. Either way, it's murder."

Yes, and she couldn't rule out the rogue gunman who was running around shooting at them. The person wearing that ski mask would have had time to set the fire before launching this latest attack against them. For that matter though, so would Mitch, Whitney and maybe even Alma.

"Wait here," Court instructed.

Since she didn't trust her legs, Rayna didn't have a choice about that. She watched as Court went into the interview room to whisper something to Egan. He was no doubt telling his brother about Bobby Joe, but Court didn't wait around for Egan's or Whitney's response. He left and went back to the squad room. A few seconds later, he returned with a bottle of water and a laptop.

In the interview room, Egan was breaking the news to Whitney, and Rayna watched the shock wash over the woman's face. More tears followed, but Rayna didn't focus on that. She turned her attention to Court, who was running a computer check on Bobby Joe's alias, Dustin Clark.

"That's all there is on him," Court said, pulling up the driver's license. "No record. Not even a parking ticket."

Probably because Bobby Joe had been living under the radar, waiting for his chance to come after her again. Of course, she still didn't know why he'd waited all this time.

"I'll check the address he gave the DMV," Court added, but he stopped when they heard the sound of voices in the squad room.

Alma.

"Why would Deputy McCall leave a message like that for me?" Alma snapped. She sounded angry. Looked it, too, when Rayna saw the woman after Court and she stepped out into the hall.

"Because I need to talk to you about a possible murder," Court answered. He sounded angry as well, but Rayna knew there was also plenty of frustration. Each thing they found only seemed to lead them to more questions.

Alma gave him a flat look. "Murder? Really? Did Warren die?"

Court matched her look with a scowl. "Not

Warren, but a man you called shortly before he was murdered."

Alma started shaking her head before he'd even finished. "The only person I've called today was one of my former hands, Dustin Clark."

Bingo. Well, at least she hadn't claimed it was a setup.

Court motioned for Alma to follow him to Egan's office, and once the three of them were inside, he shut the door. Bobby Joe's picture was still on the laptop, so Court turned it in Alma's direction.

"Is that the Dustin Clark you called?" he pressed.

Alma had a closer look at the screen. "Yes. Did something happen to him?" If she was concerned about that, she didn't show it. She could have been discussing the weather.

"He's dead. Now, tell me how you know him and why you called him. Then you can explain how you got here so fast. You didn't have enough time to drive from Durango Ridge."

"I was already here in McCall Canyon," Alma admitted. "I was coming to pay Dustin what I owed him. He's been working for me out at my ranch."

It didn't sound like a coincidence that Bobby

Joe would be working for someone with ties to the McCalls.

"There's no record of his employment with you," Court pointed out.

"Because I paid him in cash. That's the way he wanted it, and I was happy to oblige. He was good with the horses." She glanced at the screen again. "You're sure he's dead?"

"We have a body that we believe is his. When's the last time you saw him?" Court continued without even pausing.

Alma huffed, and she frowned. "Maybe about a week ago. He was at my ranch and told one of the other hands that he had to leave to take care of some personal things. He didn't come back. That's why I called him to make arrangements to meet him so I could pay him."

"And he answered that call?" Rayna wanted to know.

"Yes. Like I said, that's why I'm here in town." Alma's attention shifted back to Court. "Is this about your father?"

Court pulled back his shoulders. "Why do you ask that?"

"Because Dustin hated Warren, that's why. He never did tell me why, but a few months ago Dustin saw Warren picking me up at the ranch, and he pulled me aside later and said Warren couldn't be trusted, that he'd been a dirty cop when he was still sheriff here. I got the feeling there was some bad blood between them, but when I mentioned it to Warren, he said he didn't know anyone by that name."

And he wouldn't have, since Bobby Joe was using an alias. Still, it made Rayna wonder why Warren hadn't followed up on that. Or maybe he had so many people who disliked him that it wasn't anything that concerned him.

"Dustin's real name was Bobby Joe Hawley," Court provided. "Ever hear him mention that?"

She quickly shook her head. "I only knew him as Dustin." She stopped, looked at Rayna. "That's the man you were accused of murdering. The one that Warren was certain you'd killed," she added. "Since you were acquitted, that means you couldn't be tried for his death now."

"I didn't kill him," Rayna insisted. She kept her stare on Alma.

"Well, neither did I." Alma huffed again. "What possible motive could I have for wanting him dead?"

"Maybe you hired him to shoot my father," Court answered. "Or maybe Bobby Joe found out you'd hired someone to do that and he was trying to extort money from you. This is a long way to come to pay a ranch hand some wages. You could have just mailed him the money."

Alma's mouth tightened. "I always pay my debts." And since she'd said it through clenched teeth, it sounded like some kind of threat. But she glanced away, her expression softening a little. "Dustin… Bobby Joe or whatever his name is…said he didn't have an address here. Nor a car. He asked me to meet him."

Court and Rayna exchanged another glance, and Rayna could almost see the thought going through his head. He was wondering if Bobby Joe had been planning to set up Alma in some way. Though that still didn't explain who'd killed him.

"Bobby Joe hated my father and Rayna," Court said to Alma. "It's possible he hated them even more because she wasn't convicted of his murder. Now, think back to your dealings with Bobby Joe. Did he ever ask you any questions about Warren or Rayna?"

"Not Rayna," she answered right off. "But like I said, we did discuss Warren after he'd come to the ranch. Bobby Joe was upset, but after what I've just learned about him, maybe he was just trying to make sure Warren didn't come back. If he was supposed to be dead, he wouldn't have wanted Warren to recognize him."

True. In fact, it'd probably given Bobby Joe a jolt, or maybe a secret thrill, when he'd seen Warren.

"But Bobby Joe did mention Helen," Alma added a moment later.

Rayna saw Court's muscles go stiff, and he motioned for Alma to continue.

She did not until she'd taken a deep breath first. "It was after Warren's visit. Bobby Joe told me that Warren was married, and that his wife, Helen, was the darling of McCall Canyon. *Darling*, that's the word he used. Bobby Joe didn't come out and say it, but I could tell he suspected an affair between Warren and me." She paused. "I lied and said Warren was there on ranching business and that there was absolutely nothing going on between us."

If Bobby Joe had truly been suspicious of the affair, Rayna wondered why he hadn't exposed it. He couldn't have personally done that, but he could have sent Helen or someone else an anonymous note or maybe even pictures of Warren's visit to the Lawton ranch.

"Anyway, I told Warren it wasn't a good idea for him to visit me at my house again," Alma continued. "Warren and I ended things shortly after that."

Court stayed quiet a moment, obviously processing that. "And you didn't mention *Dustin* or what he'd said to you about my dad?"

"No." She paused again. "I didn't want to know anyone was suspicious. I mean, I could feel Warren already pulling away from me, and I didn't want to give him a reason to break things off."

That was the first time Alma had admitted that she'd wanted to stay in the relationship.

And, of course, it was also her motive for Warren's attempted murder.

It was hard for Rayna to stand there so close to the woman who might have tried to kill Court and her, but if Alma had indeed done that, then things hadn't gone according to plan. After all, Court, Warren and she were all still alive.

"Am I free to go now?" Alma asked. "Or should I call my lawyer?"

Court gave that some thought. "I don't have a reason to hold you, yet. But I'll be checking your phone records. Now would be a good time to tell me if there's something else you want to add about Bobby Joe, or anything else for that matter."

Alma's mouth tightened again. "I haven't done anything wrong, and the next time you want to speak to me, call Simon." With that, she walked out.

"You believe her?" Rayna said the moment the woman was out of the sheriff's office.

Court shrugged. "I'd love to pin this on her, but I don't think I'm objective when it comes to Alma."

No, neither was she. The woman had basically been living a lie for over thirty years, and she could be lying now.

"I meant it when I said I'll be checking out her story," Court said, "but I can do that at the ranch. I doubt you want to stay around here much longer."

She didn't. Rayna was exhausted and was now dealing with the aftereffects of the spent adrenaline. "But what about the gunman? And what with the fire and attack, I doubt Egan can spare a deputy to go with us."

"I can have a couple of the hands come here and then drive back with us. The ranch is already being guarded."

Yes, but that didn't mean it was safe. Of course, the sheriff's office wasn't exactly safe, either. Someone could easily fire shots into the building.

"Let me talk to Egan before I call the hands," Court added. But his phone rang before he could do that. "It's Larry."

Since this was the CSI, Rayna definitely wanted to hear what he had to say, and thankfully Court put the call on speaker.

"We found something," Larry said as soon as he was on the line. "Court, it's another dead body."

Chapter Fourteen

Court stared out the window of his house. It was something he did often as the sun was setting, something that usually relaxed him. But it was going to take more than familiar scenery to take this raw edge off him.

Four murders. Probably all connected, and yet they still didn't make sense. Now he could add the latest body to the "not making sense" category.

Mitch.

One of their top suspects was dead, shot at point-blank range, two bullets to the head. Since the PI and Hallie had been killed in a similar way, it was possible it'd been the same shooter. But if it was, Court didn't have any proof. All he had were those damn questions that just wouldn't stop going through his mind.

Who'd killed those people? And why? Of

course, one of the biggest questions of all—was his mother involved?

So far, Rachel hadn't found any unaccounted-for funds in Helen's checking account. No missing cash, either, from the safe at the family home. But there were other ways people could get cash. His mom could have sold some jewelry or had money stashed away that no one else had known about. The fact she'd known about the affair and had even gotten that business card from Jennifer were red flags that he couldn't ignore. The problem was it was going to be days, maybe even weeks, before he could question his mother.

"You're going to drive yourself crazy, you know that?" Rayna asked.

Her voice cut through some of his mind-clutter. So did the sound of her footsteps as she walked toward him. She'd showered and looked less tense than she had when they'd arrived back at his place. But then, if she'd looked more tense, he would have had to call the doctor because she'd been right on that edge. With reason.

She was probably the killer's next target.

Judging from the other attacks, so was he.

She came closer, and he caught the scent of the soap and shampoo she'd used. *His* soap and shampoo, but it smelled better on her than it ever had on him. She'd dressed in the jeans and blue top they'd gotten from her house. And she was holding the gun he'd given her.

The gun had been a compromise. Court hadn't wanted to give her one because he hadn't wanted her to do anything to put herself in even more danger. If there was another attack, he wanted her to get out of harm's way rather than returning fire.

But that wasn't practical.

The truth was someone could get on the ranch. Yes, the hands were watching the road, but someone could get to his house using the back trails. Heck, a gunman could climb over the fence. Rayna knew that. And that was why she now had the gun.

"Any updates?" she asked. She tucked the gun in the waistband of her jeans at the small of her back, poured herself a cup of coffee and joined him at the window.

This wasn't exactly a topic to keep her nerves steady, but Rayna needed to know. "We don't have a dental match ID on the dead guy in the car, but the other body they found is definitely Mitch. No one heard gunshots, but there was a lot of commotion what with the fire."

"Yes," she said as if giving that some thought.

"The unidentified gunman could have killed him. He could have set the fire, too."

"Or Alma or Whitney could have done it," Court quickly pointed out.

Rayna flinched, probably because it was hard for her to hear that her former friend could be a cold-blooded killer. It was especially hard since they weren't sure what Whitney's motive would have been for that.

Alma was a different story though.

"I've gone through Alma's phone records," he explained, "and she did call Bobby Joe aka Dustin three times." That wasn't a large number, and the calls could have been legit if Bobby Joe had actually been working for her.

"What about her financial records?"

He shook his head. "I haven't gotten those yet, but even when I do, I'm not expecting much. If Alma has been putting this plan together for months, then she probably would have been smart enough not to use funds that would create a money trail leading right back to her."

"True."

Court didn't think it was his imagination that she was waiting for more. "Nothing on my mother, either," he added. "Warren also hasn't been much help. He says he didn't know about Mom meeting with the PI."

"You think he could be covering for your mom? He might feel so bad about the affair that he doesn't want her punished."

That was possible, of course, but Court just couldn't buy it. "If the attacks had only been limited to Dad, he might have covered for her. *Might.* But no way would he sit back and not spill something that involved four murders. Plus, there were the attacks on us. My dad might not have valued his marriage vows, but he'd do anything to protect his kids."

She had a sip of her coffee. "You're right."

That caused him to breathe a little easier. It was already hard enough to accept his mother might have had a part in this without believing the same of his father.

"What about Bo and Whitney?" she asked. "Did Egan get anything from them when he questioned them?"

"No. Whitney stuck to her story about not having a clue what was going on. And Bo didn't say anything that he hadn't already told us. The DA plans to charge him as an adult. That might spur him to spill something new." If there was anything new to spill, that was. Bo did seem like a pawn in all of this.

Like Hallie. Maybe Jennifer, too. And since

they were both dead, it meant Bo needed to be in protective custody.

The sun finally dipped below the horizon, so Court went to the foyer, turned off the interior light and turned on the ones outside. There were about a dozen of them, and they went all around the house and grounds. When he'd had them installed though, it hadn't been with the idea of seeing an intruder. It had been to try to keep the coyotes and other wildlife away. Now it might keep that gunman from trying to sneak up on them. Just in case he did, Court made sure the security system was armed and ready. It was.

"Rachel is at the hospital with my mom," Court continued. "Egan's at the main house. Or at least he will be when he finishes up at the office."

Whenever that would be. Court figured it'd be a late night for his brother, and he was feeling guilty about that. Still, someone needed to stay with Rayna at his house, and it might as well be him.

That thought stopped him for a moment.

He *wanted* to be the one to stay with her.

Hell, that wasn't a good sign. Coupled with those kisses he'd been doling out to her, it meant he'd had a big-time loss of focus. He looked at her, to warn her about that, but one look in her eyes, and he realized no warning was necessary. Rayna knew exactly what was going on.

"Sometimes, it feels like we're back in high school," she murmured. Rayna set her coffee cup back on the counter. "Well, with the exception of someone trying to kill us, that is."

She managed to make that sound, well, light, and it caused Court to smile. She smiled, too, but then she quickly looked away as if trying to remind herself neither smiling nor looking at him that way was a good idea.

It wasn't.

Court stayed in the foyer on purpose. Best to keep some distance between them. But Rayna didn't go along with that. She went to him, her steps and body language hesitant. There was nothing hesitant about the feelings going on inside him.

He wanted her.

And no distance between them was going to remedy that. Silently cursing himself and cursing Rayna, Court strode forward to meet her and pulled her into his arms.

RAYNA HAD KNOWN the kiss was coming even before Court's mouth landed on hers. Still, she hadn't been prepared for the shock of the sensations that went through her. Yes, in some ways it did feel as if they were back in high school, but she also hadn't remembered anything this intense when they'd been teenagers.

"You know this is a big mistake, right?" Court asked when he broke away from her for air.

She did know that. So did he.

But apparently knowing wasn't going to make a difference here because he went right back for a second kiss. Rayna had been hesitant about that first one, since it'd thrown her off guard a little, but with this one, she just gave in to the moment and kissed him right back.

Rayna slid her hands around the back of his neck, pulling him closer until they were body to body. Along with the new slam of heat that gave her, it also tapped into some old memories. Of other times when Court had kissed her.

And made love to her.

He'd been her first, something she wouldn't have been able to forget even if he hadn't been doling out some mind-blowing kisses.

Court stopped again, easing back so they could make eye contact. It seemed to be his way of giving her an out. He was giving her time to put a stop to this. But Rayna had no intentions of stopping it. That was why she pulled him right back to her.

He deepened the kiss, stoking the fire between them. And he stoked it even more when he took those kisses to her neck. It didn't take her body long to realize it wanted a lot more of what Court was giving her.

Years ago, Court and she had kissed like this for hours, driving each other crazy, until they'd finally become lovers. All of that came back now and upped the urgency even more.

She reached for the buttons on his shirt, but his hands got in the way. That was because he pulled off her top, tossing it onto the floor. In the same motion, he kissed her breasts. First, the tops, and then he shoved down her bra to kiss her the way Rayna wanted. He'd remembered those were sensitive spots for her, and he made sure he gave her as much pleasure as possible.

But soon, it wasn't enough.

Rayna went after his shirt again and managed to get enough buttons undone so she could kiss his chest. Apparently, that upped the urgency for him, too, because Court pulled her to the floor.

There were no lights on inside, but the exterior lights were enough for Rayna to see his face. Mercy, he was hot. Always had been, and that hadn't changed. If anything, the years had made him even better, and she regretted the time she'd lost with him.

Regretted, too, that she might never have him again like that.

That tugged at her heart, but Rayna didn't have time to dwell on it. That was because the kisses continued. The touches, too, but it was obvious that foreplay wasn't going to last much longer. That was okay with Rayna. For now, she just needed Court to soothe the fierce ache inside her. She needed him to make her forget all the bad things that had been happening.

Of course, she wouldn't forget for long, but that didn't matter.

All that mattered right now was having him.

Court did his part to speed things along. He took out her gun, placing it on the floor next to them, and he shimmied her out of her jeans. Since he'd already taken off her bra and top, it made her aware of just how naked she was. He wasn't. So, she rid him of his shirt and tackled ridding him of the rest of his clothes.

It wasn't pretty, but she was about to get

him unzipped and shove off his jeans when he stopped her by sliding his hand over hers.

"Condom," he managed to say. He rummaged through his back pocket to get his wallet and took out a condom from it.

She groaned because she hadn't even remembered safe sex. Then she groaned again, this time in pleasure, when Court started kissing her again.

Those wildfire kisses didn't make it easier for her to move around, but Rayna managed to get him unzipped, and Court broke the kiss long enough to put on the condom.

He looked at her again, and Rayna thought maybe she saw some hesitation in his eyes. But no. There was no hesitation whatsoever when he pushed into her.

She got another huge jolt of pleasure, and it just kept coming when Court started to move inside her. This was familiar but also new. He'd obviously learned more about how to please a woman since their make-out sessions in high school. He seemed to know just how to touch her. Just how to move. Just how to make her crazy with need.

The need couldn't last, of course. That meant the pleasure couldn't, either.

When the pace became harder and faster, it

pushed Rayna right over the edge. There was nothing she could do but hold on to Court and make sure he went over the edge with her.

Chapter Fifteen

"I'm getting too old for floor sex," Court grumbled.

Though it really wasn't much of a complaint. His body was slack and practically humming, but if Rayna and he stayed on the hardwood floor much longer, that slackness was going to be replaced with some back aches. That was why he got up, scooped her up in his arms and carried her to the bedroom.

Rayna made a sleepy moan of pleasure and kissed him before he headed to the bathroom. Once he was done, he fully intended to slide right into bed with Rayna and maybe make another mistake tonight.

And it had been a mistake.

Still, he wasn't seeing how he was going to stop himself from making another one. He wanted her, and Court doubted anyone would be able to talk him out of that. Maybe Rayna would get a sudden dose of common sense and tell him to go back to keeping watch.

Or not.

When he went into the bedroom, she patted the spot next to her, motioning for him to join her. She also had a sly smile on her face. Couple with the fact that she was naked, and it erased any chance of him putting a stop to this.

He got on the bed, automatically pulling her into his arms and kissing her. The kiss would have gone on a lot longer if he hadn't heard the ringing sound. It wasn't in his head, either. It was coming from his phone, which he'd left in the foyer. Since it could be a critical call, he bolted from the bed and ran to get it.

Rachel's name was on the screen.

"Is everything okay?" Court immediately asked.

"Fine. Well, you know that's a lie. What I should say is that Mom and I are safe. What about Rayna and you?"

"We're safe, too," he settled for saying.

He really wanted to enjoy seeing Rayna naked a while longer, but when she came into the foyer to gather up her clothes and start dressing, Court did the same. He also put the call on speaker for her.

"Good." Rachel hesitated, and Court wondered if his sister had sensed what'd just gone on. If she did though, she didn't mention it. "Mom is all settled in her room here. It looks like a regular hospital room, but it's, well, noisy. Lots of people coming and going, and every now and then I can hear someone shout. Apparently, they have patients in here who get agitated easily."

His sister wasn't painting a good picture of the place, but maybe his mom wouldn't have to be there for long. "What about security?"

"There's a Texas Ranger in the hall and another out front. I've come to the cafeteria for a while so we can talk about that business card she had. Mom's been sedated since we got here, but I asked her if she hired someone." Rachel paused. "She did. His name is Abraham Stigler. But she insists he didn't really do much for her."

Court replayed that last bit word for word. "But he did do something?"

He could hear more chatter along with Rachel's frustrated breath. "Stigler apparently wanted to try to lure Dad into a compromising position with Alma so he could get photographs. Of course, Stigler wanted her to use those pictures to launch into a divorce where Mom could get a better settlement than she otherwise would have gotten. Mom refused. Stigler got mad and stormed off."

He definitely didn't like the sound of that. "Is it possible this Stigler is unhinged? Because that doesn't sound like the behavior of a professional PI. If so, he could be the triggerman in these attacks."

"I asked Mom about that in a roundabout way, but she didn't think he would do anything violent. She said he was just frustrated that she was going to let herself be treated like that. Apparently, his dad cheated on his mom, so it's a sore spot for him. Anyway, I've got my laptop here, so I did some checking and didn't find anything on him, either."

That didn't mean there wasn't something to find. "Thanks, sis. I'll let you know if I come up with anything. Try to get some rest," he added.

Since checking on the PI could take a while, Court gave Rayna another kiss. One that he hoped would let her know that…except he didn't know what he wanted her to know. That was because he didn't have a clue where this was going. Worse, he really didn't have time to figure it out.

"Work on the PI," Rayna prompted. "I'll make a fresh pot of coffee."

Coffee wasn't much of a substitute for kissing, sex or even a "where is this going?" discussion, but she was right. It could wait.

Court called the sheriff's office to get someone to access the computer, and Ian answered. However, Ian spoke before Court could say anything.

"I was about to call you. The dead guy in the car had a receipt in his wallet. One for the Lone Star Inn here in town. The CSIs found out that a person matching Bobby Joe's description had a room there, and they're going through it now. Court, they found something."

Judging from Ian's tone, that *something* wasn't good. He tried to steel himself, and he waited for Ian to continue. He didn't have to wait long.

"The dead guy has to be Bobby Joe because he has some recordings saved on a laptop, and I'm emailing them to you now so you can see for yourself," Ian explained. "Uh, is Rayna with you?"

"Yes."

"Okay. Well, the recordings will probably upset her. Just thought you should know that up front."

Hell. Court wished there was a way to keep this from her, but he couldn't. After everything

Bobby Joe had put her through, she deserved to know the truth.

Since it sounded as if Ian had his hands full, Court decided to wait on having the deputy check on the PI. Instead, he ended the call, and with Rayna right there next to him, he went to his laptop and accessed the file. It didn't take long for the images to appear on the screen.

Bobby Joe.

Yeah, it was him all right. Court could tell that even though Bobby Joe wasn't looking directly into the camera. He had also grown a beard. Court checked the date on the recording, and it'd been made just three days ago. Or rather that was when it'd been uploaded.

"It's time to make Rayna pay," Bobby Joe said. He was resting against the headboard of a bed and drinking a beer. "Revenge is best served up cold, you know."

Someone else in the room said something that Court couldn't hear. It was a mumble, and whoever had said it wasn't on the screen.

"Because she made a promise to love me forever, that's why," Bobby Joe snapped in response to whatever the other person had said. There was pure venom in his tone. "That's what you promise when you accept a marriage proposal. It's like a lie when you break a promise, and no one's gonna get away with lying to me."

Rayna's breathing became faster, and she inched closer to the screen. "I'm not sure he knows he's being recorded."

Neither was Court, but he was surprised that Rayna could pick up on that, considering the hatred in Bobby Joe's voice.

The other person mumbled something else, something that caused Bobby Joe to bolt up from the headboard. "It matters," he snarled. "It was fun, watching her always looking over her shoulder. Living like a monk because she was too scared I'd come jumping out at her."

Rayna shuddered, and Court knew why. This meant Bobby Joe had indeed been watching her all this time.

"Rayna's gonna have to pay," Bobby Joe grumbled after downing some more beer. "I'm gonna burn that bitch alive."

That was obviously a little more than Rayna could take because she dropped back a step. Court slipped his arm around her. It wasn't much, but then there wasn't much they could do except finish listening to what this snake had to say.

"That'll teach her to file charges against me,"

Bobby Joe went on with his rant. "That'll teach her what happens when she breaks a promise."

The recording ended, but it was more than enough to let Court know that Bobby Joe had indeed been out to kill Rayna.

"Someone intentionally left this recording for us to find," Court said.

"Yes." She agreed so quickly that it meant she'd come to the same conclusion. "Is there any chance there can be a voice analysis done on the other person in the room with him?"

"Maybe." And considering this had been recorded three days ago, it could have been any of their suspects. "Ian's probably already sent it to the Ranger Crime Lab, but I'll make sure." He paused. "Whoever was in that room, Bobby Joe felt comfortable enough with him or her to admit to conspiracy to commit murder."

She nodded. "Plus, the recording might not even be recent." Rayna motioned toward the background of the shot Court had frozen on the screen. "I've never been to the inn, but I'm not even sure that's where this was recorded."

No, and if it hadn't been, maybe someone had planted the laptop with the recording in the room. For that matter, the person could have planted the receipt, as well.

Court's phone rang, and with all the things

that'd been going on, he expected it to be Ian calling with more bad news of something they'd found at the inn. But it wasn't. It was Rachel.

Since his sister could have her own version of bad news, something else she'd perhaps learned from their mother, Court took a deep breath before he answered.

"You have to come right away," Rachel said, her voice filled with panic. "Mom's missing. I just got back to her room, and she's not here. God, Court, I think someone kidnapped her."

RAYNA KNEW THIS could be some kind of setup. A ruse to get Court and her out of his house. But the problem was, it was going to work.

Because there was no chance Court was going to stay put if his mother was in some kind of danger. That was why they'd practically run to his cruiser when they'd heard what Rachel said, and Court had started driving the moment they were inside. He'd also had Rayna use her phone to call Ian and tell the deputy to meet them on the road that led from the ranch to San Antonio. That way, they would at least have some backup.

"Rachel, tell me exactly what happened,"

Court insisted. He still had her on the line, and he'd put the call on speaker.

His sister didn't answer right away though, something she'd been doing since her bombshell of Helen being gone. That was because Rachel was also answering frantic questions from people who most likely were the staff and the Texas Ranger.

"Rachel?" Court said in a much louder voice.

He wasn't panicking like his sister, but he wasn't exactly cool and calm, either. That lack of calmness wasn't just limited to his mom though. His gaze fired all around them, keeping watch, and he motioned for Rayna to do the same. She did, and she also kept a firm grip on the gun he'd given her.

She prayed she didn't have to use it, but it was nearly an hour's drive to San Antonio, and plenty could go wrong between here and there. Maybe it wouldn't take Ian long to join them. Of course, someone could attack them while Ian was with them, but at least they'd have an extra gun if things went wrong.

"No, I don't know where she went," she heard Rachel say. "I've already told you that a dozen times. Now find her." Rachel made a hoarse sound before she came back on the phone. "Court, I don't know where she is.

They think I helped her escape, but I wouldn't do that."

"I believe you. Now, tell me what happened."

"I'm not sure." Rachel made another of those sobbing sounds. "I was in the cafeteria making some other calls, and when I came back to her room, Mom wasn't there."

"But you said you thought someone kidnapped her," Court pointed out.

"Someone did. I should have never left her alone."

"You thought she was safe. You didn't do anything wrong," Court said, and he somehow managed to speak calmly. "What about the Ranger? Who is he and how did someone get past him?" His voice got a little harder on those two questions.

It took Rachel a moment to answer. "The Ranger's name is Marcus Owen, and he said someone dressed like a janitor walked past him and hit him with a stun gun. After he was down, the guy used pepper spray on him."

That tightened Rayna's chest. The memories of her own attack came flooding back, and the man who'd gone after her had used a stun gun, too. No pepper spray, but Helen McCall hadn't gotten a syringe of drugs pumped into her. "Mom's room is a mess, like there was some kind of a struggle," Rachel said. "Items had been knocked off the stand next to her bed. Her things are still here, so I don't think robbery was the motive."

Neither did Rayna. "What about the Ranger? Did he see the face of the man who used the stun gun on him?"

"I don't think so. Ranger Owen's still coughing from the pepper spray, so he might remember more once his head is clearer."

Court cursed. "What about security cameras? They should be all over that place."

"They are, and someone's trying to get the surveillance footage from them now. The ones in the parking lot, too."

That was a start, but even if they could identify the guy, it didn't mean they could stop him. By now, he could have already taken Helen out of the hospital. Plus, since the woman had been sedated, it was possible she wouldn't be able to figure out a way to escape. Even if she did fight off the sedation, her attacker could obviously use the stun gun or pepper spray on her.

"Mom must have screamed or something," Court added. "No way would she just let a stranger take her."

"She wouldn't have. I think that's why the

room looks as if it's been trashed. Oh, God. Court, you don't think he would hurt her, do you?"

"No, I don't," Court quickly answered, but judging from his suddenly tight jaw muscles and the death grip that he had on the steering wheel, he was considering the same thing.

"Whoever took her probably wants to use her for leverage," Rayna suggested. "That means he won't hurt her."

"Leverage for what?" Rachel asked.

"I'm not sure," Rayna lied. But she had a strong inkling this was either tied to Warren or Court and her. "Did you let your dad know what's going on?"

"I called his guard," Rachel said. "I wanted to make sure he hadn't been taken, too, but he's okay. I told the guards to make sure it stayed that way."

"Thanks for doing that," Court told her. "Are the local cops out looking for this guy who took Mom?"

"I think so. If not, Egan will make sure they are when he gets here. How long before you can come?"

"I'm on the way now. Whatever you do, don't leave the hospital, and don't go looking for Mom. Just stay put until Egan and I get there, and we can figure out what to do. Don't worry, we'll get Mom back."

Rayna knew that Court would do anything in his power to make that happen, but this might be beyond what he could do. She hadn't wanted to mention it with Rachel on the phone, but the moment Court ended the call, she knew she had to say something.

"This could turn into some kind of ransom demand," Rayna told him.

Court nodded. "For either us or Dad." He cursed again and continued to keep watch. "There's another thing to consider. We're not sure that burned body is actually Bobby Joe. He could be the one behind this."

"Yes," she admitted, "but that doesn't explain the recording on the laptop." Rayna hated to even consider that Bobby Joe might be innocent in this, but she had to force herself to at least consider it. "The recording on the laptop could have been made years ago, and now someone could be using it to set up Bobby Joe."

"I agree," Court answered several moments later. "Since someone used Hallie to try to set you up and then murdered her, the person could have done the same to Bobby Joe."

She hated Bobby Joe for what he'd done to

her, but he didn't deserve to be murdered. If that was what had happened. It was entirely possible that the body in the car wasn't his. Maybe it belonged to someone else that this unidentified killer had eliminated to tie up some loose ends.

"Call Ian so we can find out his location," Court instructed.

Rayna did, putting the call on speaker and holding the phone so that Court would be able to speak to his fellow deputy. Ian answered on the first ring.

"We're about five miles from the exit to the highway," Court said abruptly.

"I'm on my way there now, too. I should arrive in just a couple of minutes. If I make it ahead of you, I'll wait."

"Good." Court opened his mouth to say more, but he stopped. "What the hell?" he grumbled, and he hit his brakes.

It took Rayna a moment to realize why he'd done that. It was because someone had stretched a spike strip across the road. It was the kind of thing that cops used to stop bad guys from getting away. They ran right over it, the spikes tearing through the tires.

The cruiser jolted from the impact, and

Rayna immediately felt something she didn't want to feel.

The tires were quickly going flat.

And that made Court and her sitting ducks.

COURT DIDN'T TAKE the time to curse, but that was what he'd do later. For now though, he got the cruiser to the side of the road so he could stop and draw his gun. Rayna had hers ready, and like him, she was looking all around, trying to find out who'd just set this trap for them.

"What happened?" Ian said from the other end of the line.

"Spike strip. Head this way, but approach with caution. I'm betting the person who put it there is still around."

Rayna pulled in a hard breath. Of course, she'd already known that, but it was probably unsettling to hear it said aloud.

"I'll get there as fast as I can," Ian assured him.

Court ended the call and put his phone back in his pocket. That way, he'd be ready when Ian arrived. He didn't want anything slowing him down when he moved Rayna from his cruiser to Ian's.

"Do you see anything?" she asked. Her voice was shaky, but he had to hand it to her, she was looking and sounding stronger than he'd expected. He hoped that she wasn't actually getting used to being put in danger like this.

"No," Court answered.

But it was hard to see much of anything. There was only a sliver of a moon, and even though the headlights were cutting through the darkness, that allowed them to see only directly ahead. It was pitch-dark behind them. It also didn't help that there were ditches and plenty of trees in the pastures on both sides of them. It'd be easy for someone to hide out there and wait to attack.

"No way could the person who took Mom have made it out here already," Court said.

He was talking more to himself than Rayna. But it could mean that the man who'd previously attacked them wasn't behind this. Well, he wasn't if he'd been the one to take Helen.

"It could be another hired gun," Rayna muttered.

Yeah. A hired gun who was enjoying watching them squirm. Now that their car was disabled, why hadn't the person come after them? Why wait when he or she would know that backup had to be on the way?

His phone rang again, and Court glanced at the screen to see Rachel's name there. He was debating whether or not he should answer when he saw something. A blur of motion to their right, on the passenger's side of the cruiser.

Someone was in the pasture.

"Get down on the seat," he told Rayna.

"You need me to keep watch," she argued.

He hated that she was right. Hated even more that he might need her help to get out of this.

Rayna already followed his gaze to the pasture, but Court could no longer see anyone moving out there. He kept watch. Not just there, but he looked around them, too, in case there was more than one person involved in this.

"There," Rayna said. She motioned toward the road just ahead. "I think someone just got in that ditch."

Court hadn't seen it, but it was possible, especially since the headlights weren't focused on the ditch. He put the cruiser into Drive, knowing he wouldn't get far, but he wanted to move the vehicle only enough to shine some light in that specific area.

And it worked.

He saw the person then. Whoever it was, he or she was definitely in the ditch.

"I could lower my window enough to try to get off a shot," Rayna suggested.

But he was already shaking his head before she even finished speaking. "Not a chance. Just keep watch to the side and behind us." That way, he could deal with this snake.

The windows were bullet resistant. That was both the good and the bad news. It meant the guy in the ditch wouldn't be able to execute an immediate kill shot. He'd have to fire enough to tear through the glass. But it also meant Court wouldn't have an easy shot, either.

Even though it was a risk, he lowered his window a couple of inches and aimed his gun out the narrow space. He put his finger on the trigger.

And he waited, his attention nailed to the spot where he'd last seen the person. He doubted this was some hunter or innocent bystander out for an evening stroll. No, this was the person who'd put out the spike strip. The person who probably wanted them dead.

The seconds crawled by, but it didn't take him long to get a whiff of something in the air.

Gasoline.

Rayna obviously smelled it, too, because she practically snapped her head in his direction.

"It could be coming from the cruiser," he told her.

Though there was a slim to none chance of that being the case. Still, Court held out hope that maybe the spike strip had somehow flipped up when he'd driven over it and punctured the gas line.

His phone rang, and again it was Rachel. It was a bad time to be talking on the phone, but Court hit the speaker button anyway.

"We got a call," Rachel blurted out the moment he answered. "God, Court. It's really bad."

His chest went so tight that it was hard for him to breathe. "Is Mom okay?"

"I don't know. The caller said he'll exchange her for Rayna."

That definitely didn't help with the tightness. "I want that call traced."

"Ranger Owen's trying to do that now." His sister sounded even more desperate now than she had earlier. "The kidnapper said he'd kill Mom if we didn't hand over Rayna in thirty minutes."

"I can't get there that soon," Rayna said, and Court knew then that she was indeed planning on surrendering to the kidnapper to save his mother.

"There's no guarantee the kidnapper will let either you or my mother live," Court pointed out.

"We have to try. Someone disabled Court's cruiser," Rayna said in a louder voice to Rachel. "But as soon as Ian is here, I can get to San Antonio. Tell the kidnapper when he calls back."

Rayna looked at Court. "We have to try to save your mother."

Court was certain he would have come up with an argument for that, but he saw the headlights ahead. Then his phone dinged with a message from Ian.

"Rachel, I have to call you back," Court insisted, and he switched his screen to the text.

Is it safe to approach? Ian texted.

No, it wasn't. Someone's in the ditch to your left, Court answered back.

He waited for Ian's response, and since Ian was a lot closer to that particular section of the ditch, he might be able to see the person. The moment that thought crossed his mind, there was another blur of motion.

Then Court heard the swooshing sound.

As a wall of fire shot up right in front of them.

Chapter Sixteen

From the moment the cruiser had hit the spike strip, Rayna had known they were in trouble. Now that trouble had just escalated.

"I can't drive off because of the flat tires," Court grumbled under his breath, and he cursed.

No, and that meant if the fire started to come toward them, they would have no choice but to get out of the cruiser and run. That would no doubt make it much easier for them to be gunned down.

If the smoke and fire didn't get to them first, that was.

Because of the direction of the wind, the smoke started to come right at them. Using the cruiser's AC would help, but not for long. Worse, the smoke was making it very hard to see anything.

Court's phone rang. It was Ian, and he answered it without taking his eyes off their surroundings.

"I'm going to try to drive through the fire to get to you," Ian said. "Maybe the flames will conceal you enough so you can jump in."

He didn't sound very hopeful about that, and neither was Rayna. Any hope whatsoever vanished when there was a gunshot. It was a loud blast, and judging from the sound, it went in the direction of Ian's cruiser. A few seconds later, another sound followed the gunfire.

The hiss from the new flames that flared up between Ian and them.

Also on the side of them, too.

The ditch across from the driver's side of the cruiser burst on fire, too.

Now there were two new walls of flames and smoke, these latest ones even higher than the first. That would make it too dangerous for Ian to drive through it because if he got stuck, it could cause his gas tank to explode.

Court cursed again, and he started coughing. "Whoever's behind this had to have put more than just accelerant on the road. There has to be incendiary devices."

Yes, ones that were probably operated by remote control, since Rayna didn't see anyone close enough to set the fire by hand. However, the person had to be nearby, waiting for them.

And Rayna didn't have to guess the location. There was only one path—to her right—that wasn't on fire, and that was almost certainly where their attacker wanted them to go. It meant that was where an ambush had to be waiting for them.

The smoke started to smother her and burn her eyes. Again, it was exactly what their attacker wanted. They couldn't sit there much longer.

"I called the fire department," Ian said. His voice was laced with frustration and fear, and he was also coughing from the smoke. "When they get here, they might be able to get close enough to put out the flames."

Not likely, since they wouldn't be able to approach if there was gunfire.

And that meant Court, Ian and she had to figure out a way to find the fire starter and take him or her out of commission. If the fire jumped the road and ditch, it could start burning the pastures and the nearby ranches. Of course, that didn't seem so urgent as the danger that was right on top of them.

"Can you go in reverse?" Court asked Ian.

"I can, but I'd rather get closer to Rayna and you. I can maybe help you."

"That's too risky," Court warned him. "Put some distance between the fire and you."

"I'll try... Wait, I've got another call coming in," Ian said.

So did Court. It was Rachel again, and Rayna could see that he was hesitant about answering it. She knew why, too. He probably didn't want to tell his sister about their situation. Rachel was already frantic enough about their mother, and hearing this wasn't going to help. Still. Court hit the answer button, and as he'd done with Ian, he put it on speaker and continued to keep watch.

"Where are you?" Rachel blurted out.

Court hesitated, obviously trying to figure out how to say this. "Rayna, Ian and I are trapped on the road. Someone set fires, and that means I'm not going to be able to get to you right away."

A sob caught in Rachel's throat. "Are you okay?"

He didn't even attempt a lie. "No. If the kidnapper calls back, negotiate for more time for Mom. I'll call you when I can."

Court ended the call just as another wave of smoke came at them. Now it was impossible to see anything, and even though the flames weren't advancing on them, the cruiser was getting hotter with each passing second.

"We can't stay here." Court looked Rayna straight in the eyes when he said that, and she saw the apology that she hoped he wouldn't say.

Because this wasn't his fault.

It was the fault of that snake out there who'd put all of this together. Rayna only hoped she learned the reason for all of this. While she was hoping, she also wanted to catch the person and put an end to this danger once and for all.

"What do you need me to do?" Rayna asked before Court could add that *I'm sorry*.

"Put your phone in your pocket so you don't lose it and then switch places with me," he said through the coughs. He tipped his head to the ditch on the passenger's side of the cruiser. "I'll go out first. You'll be right behind me. We'll take cover and try to shoot this guy before he shoots us."

It was a simple enough plan, and they might get lucky. *Might*. But there were plenty of things that could go wrong. As thick as the smoke was, their attacker could be already waiting right outside the door, and Court and she wouldn't know it until it was too late.

Court sent a text to Ian, no doubt to tell him what they were about to do. Maybe Ian would be able to help in some way, but at this point, the deputy just needed to figure out a way to get out of that fire and be safe.

Rayna pushed back the seat as far as it would go to give Court space to maneuver. It wasn't easy now that they were coughing nonstop. Plus, Rayna felt on the verge of panicking. It was hard to breathe with the rising heat and the adrenaline. Even harder to catch her breath when Court brushed a quick kiss on her mouth.

"Stay safe," he said.

She repeated that to him and prayed that both of them and Ian could manage to do just that.

Court threw open the cruiser door, and they immediately caught another wave of the smoke. No bullets though, so maybe the visibility wasn't so good for the shooter, either.

Using the door for cover, Court got out, and while staying in a crouched position, he inched closer to the ditch. He glanced around, but she could tell from the way he was blinking that the smoke was doing a number on his eyes.

"Let's move now," he whispered.

He took hold of her wrist, pulled Rayna out of the cruiser. In the same motion, he hurried toward the ditch. They didn't make it far.

Before the shot came right at them.

COURT SHOVED RAYNA into the ditch as fast as he could, but it hadn't been quite fast enough.

The shot slammed into the ground, kicking up the dirt and sending some of it into his eyes. Not good. He was already having a hard enough time seeing as it was. And now his heart was beating so fast that it felt as if his ribs might crack. That was because he wasn't sure if the bullet had ricocheted and hit Rayna.

She could be hurt.

Rayna made a sharp sound of pain, and Court caught her in his arms, dropping down as far as they could go. The ditch was soft from the recent rain, and it helped break their fall a little. Still, it was a hard landing.

"I'm okay," Rayna said. Though she certainly didn't sound okay. "I just hit my head."

That wasn't good, since she already had an injury there, but it was better than the alternative. They could have been shot. Hell. How had he allowed it to come to this?

Because he was stupid, that was why.

He'd let the news of his mother's disappearance cloud his mind, and now Rayna might pay for that mistake.

Since he didn't know where the shooter was, Court adjusted his position so that Rayna's back was against the side of the ditch and he was in front of her and facing the pasture. The lower ground helped with the smoke, too, and thankfully the wind seemed to be blowing some of it away. That was a good thing because he needed to be able to catch his breath in case they had to run.

Court tried to pick through the smoke and darkness to spot their attacker. Nothing. Nor did the person fire any other shots. Normally, that would have been a good thing, but it could mean the person was moving closer—maybe trying to get in place for a kill shot.

His phone buzzed with a text message. It was Ian, again. But Court didn't answer it. He didn't want to be distracted even for a second, so he passed it to Rayna so she could read it to him.

"Ian says he's going to try to go back up the road and find a way to get into the pasture where we are," she whispered.

That was beyond risky, but at this point, everything they did fell into that category. If Court had been alone, he would have told Ian to get to safety, but since Rayna was involved, Court was willing to take all the help he could get.

Behind them, the fire snapped and hissed, but it didn't seem to be burning itself out. Not good. Because the flames could still reach the gas tank on the cruiser. If it exploded, Rayna and he were plenty close enough to be hurt or killed.

"We have to move," he said, keeping his voice as soft as he could manage. And there was only one direction in which to do that. Too bad it would mean moving away from Ian, but he had to get Rayna away from the fire. "Stay behind me and try to keep watch," he added.

She nodded, and he could feel the tightness in her body. Her too-fast breath on his neck. As a lawman, he'd faced danger, but Rayna shouldn't have to be going through this. Unfortunately, they didn't have a choice about that right now.

With him still in front of her, they started moving to their right. Inch by inch. It was very slow going because they had to stay crouched down. They made it about two feet before Court saw something.

A person darted behind a tree directly in front of them.

Because of the smoke, he couldn't tell if the person was a man or a woman, but he definitely saw the gun. A rifle. If it had a scope, which it probably did, it was going to make it much easier to target Rayna and him. Court instantly got proof that he'd been right.

The next bullet tore into the ditch, and if Rayna and he hadn't ducked down, it would have hit them. That was way too close for comfort.

It didn't stay just one shot, either. A second one came. Then a third. All of them were ripping into the dirt just above them. Court had no choice but to pull Rayna back down to the ground. That meant he no longer had a visual on the shooter.

Behind them, he heard another hissing sound, and almost immediately new flames shot into the air. This fire was even bigger than the others and jumped up right next to the ditch. If the ground caved in any more from the shots, it would send that fire spilling down on them.

"How much ammo do you have?" Rayna asked.

That wasn't a question he especially wanted to hear. Because it sounded as if she was thinking about doing something he wouldn't like.

"I have two extra magazines plus what's in my gun," Court answered. "Why?"

"Because we can't stay here. If we can pin down this guy, then we can get farther down the ditch and away from the smoke and heat."

She was right about the "staying here" part, but there was no way he wanted her high enough out of the ditch to return fire. But he did have an idea.

A risky one.

It might work though if there was only one shooter. If there were more than that, well, things were going to go from bad to worse.

Still, it wasn't as if they had many options here, and those options decreased when their attacker started sending more shots their way. Each bullet was slamming into the very dirt that could bury them in that fire.

Court tipped his head to their right. "Stay low but move as fast as you can," he told Rayna.

He couldn't see her expression, but he felt her tense even more—something that he hadn't thought was possible. "What about you?" Her voice was shaking now, too.

"I'll be right behind you."

Or at least he would be once he was certain he'd pinned down the shooter enough for him to do that. For now, his goal was just to get Rayna as far away from that fire as he could manage.

He doubted she believed that "right behind you" part, but she moved out from behind him. "Just be careful," she whispered.

Court nodded, told her to do the same. "Go now," he instructed.

He came out from cover, lifting his head and gun high enough so he could send a shot in the general direction where he'd pinpointed the shooter.

The gunman fired back.

Court dropped down, and from the corner of his eye he saw Rayna doing exactly what he wanted her to do. She was practically on all fours and was scrambling down the ditch away from him. She wasn't nearly far enough though, so he came out from cover and fired another shot.

That was when Court finally got a glimpse of the shooter. The person immediately darted behind a tree that was about twenty yards from them. Unfortunately, there were plenty of trees and underbrush on each side of their attacker, so Court had no way of knowing which way he would go.

There was a slash of bright lights to his left, and Court whipped his gun in that direction.

But he didn't think it was a gunman. It was hard to tell with the smoke, but he thought it might be Ian, and that he might be seeing the headlights from the cruiser.

Court glanced at Rayna again. She was still moving. Still staying down. And so the shooter would stay pinned down, too, Court fired another shot where he'd last spotted him.

Nothing.

He doubted that meant the guy had just left, though it was possible the headlights had given him second thoughts about leaning out to shoot.

The lights came closer. Yeah, it was Ian all right. Maybe the deputy would get in position to help them. But that hope barely had time to register in Court's mind when there was another hissing sound.

Much, much louder than the others. The flames came. Not just on the road this time, either.

But into the ditch.

The line of fire flared between Rayna and him. And the flames came right at Court.

Chapter Seventeen

"Watch out!" Rayna called out to Court.

But it was too late.

She'd seen the new flash of fire, but she hadn't been able to warn Court in time for him to get out of the way. Rayna turned to hurry back to him, and that was when she realized she couldn't.

Because the line of fire was coming in her direction, too.

Whoever had set this latest fire had obviously meant to burn Court and her alive in the ditch. Well, Rayna had no plans to die, and she wanted to make sure Court didn't, either.

Since she couldn't move very fast on all fours, she got to her feet and started running. She hated putting more distance between Court and her, but maybe she'd be able to get into the pasture and then double back for him. Something that he was hopefully doing as well, since Rayna didn't want him staying near that fire. Of course, being in the pasture wouldn't exactly be safe, either.

The line of fire finally stopped moving behind her. Probably because there was no more accelerant to fuel the flames. She stopped and ducked back down in the ditch. Low enough for cover but high enough so she could try to spot the shooter.

Nothing.

The smoke and darkness were acting like a thick, smothering curtain all around her. Worse, the sound of fire might be able to mask the footsteps of anyone trying to sneak up on her. That was why she stayed facing the pasture. If the attacker came at her, that was the direction he'd likely come from.

Rayna could see the headlights from Ian's cruiser to her left, but she had no idea where the deputy was. Maybe Court would be able to get to him, and they could use the cruiser to come after her. At least then they'd be protected from gunfire.

Her phone buzzed with a text, and even though it meant taking her eyes off the pasture, she glanced down at the screen, since it could be important.

It was.

Get as far away from the fire as you can, Court texted her. *I'll come for you soon.*

Despite their god-awful situation, relief flooded through her. Court was okay. For now, anyway. Rayna prayed that it stayed that way. But it didn't last.

A shot blasted through the air.

The bullet wasn't fired in her direction though but rather had gone near Court. She doubted either Court or Ian had fired it, since it'd seemed to come from the area by the trees.

There was another shot.

Then another.

Rayna ducked down even farther into the ditch, but with the fourth shot, she was better able to pinpoint the location of the shooter. The person was moving away from Court and in her direction. Since the line of trees continued almost to the ditch, she had to keep watch not just in front of her but also to the side.

In the distance she heard sirens. Probably from the fire department. They wouldn't be able to help, but at least they'd be close enough to put out the fires once the shooter was no longer a threat. Whenever that would be.

Her phone dinged again. It wasn't from Court this time but rather from Ian. And the message he sent her had her stomach going straight to her knees.

Court was hit, Ian texted.

Rayna forced herself not to scream and bolt from the ditch to hurry to him. That was exactly what the shooter wanted her to do, and he would almost certainly gun her down. But while she could make herself stay put, she couldn't stop the strangled groan that made its way through her throat.

No. This couldn't be happening.

Somehow, she had to get to him, had to help him, but she couldn't just go running into the pasture. Rayna forced herself to stop, and breathe, so she could try to think this through. It was hard to think though with the worst-case scenarios going through her head. And that was when she realized something.

She was in love with Court.

That was why she was reacting this way. That was why losing him suddenly seemed unbearable.

Maybe part of her always had been in love with him, but it had taken something like this to make her see it. Now she might not even get the chance to tell him how she felt.

How bad is he hurt? Rayna texted back. No

way could she ask if Court was dead. She refused to believe that could happen.

The seconds crawled by, turning into what felt an eternity. Because her legs suddenly felt as if they couldn't support her weight, Rayna leaned her back against the wall of the ditch. And waited. Even though she was expecting it, the jolt of surprise still went through her when her phone dinged.

Court says it's not bad, that it's just a flesh wound, Ian finally answered. He'll be okay.

Rayna had no idea if that was true or if Court was merely trying to prevent her from panicking. If so, it wasn't working.

Can you get Court into the cruiser? she texted Ian.

She didn't have to wait nearly as long for a response. No. We tried to get to it, and that's how he got shot. But Court wants me to try to get to you.

Of course he did. But Rayna had to nix that with a semi-lie of her own. I'm safe where I am, she answered.

She definitely didn't want Ian leaving Court alone, especially since Court might not be able to defend himself.

Thea and John will be here soon, Ian added a moment later.

Good. Two more deputies might help them put an end to this. Again though, they might not be able to get close because of the fire.

Rayna slipped her phone back in her pocket so she could free up her hands, and she looked around the pasture again. There was no more gunfire, no glimpse of anyone in the trees. That didn't mean someone wasn't out there, but for now they were staying hidden.

That surprised her.

She would have thought the shooter would have wanted to go ahead and put an end to this, since he had to know that backup was on the way. Maybe it meant the guy had pulled the plug on this attack and had fled. Even though she wanted to catch this snake, right now her priority was helping Court.

When the next minute crawled by without any other gunfire, Rayna figured it was now or never for her to get to Court. Since she couldn't risk the pasture in front of her, that meant taking an alternate route. She could hurry into the pasture on the other side of the road, skirting along the edges of the fire until she could get to a clearing to cross back over.

She got her gun ready and looked over her shoulder at the road behind her. The only thing she could see was thick smoke, and Rayna knew the moment she stepped into it, she'd start coughing, something that would slow her down. That was why she took a deep breath and turned to scramble out of the ditch.

But turning was as far as she got.

Someone wearing a gas mask reached out from that smoke, and that someone had a stun gun. Before Rayna could move or make a sound, the person rammed the gun against her neck.

The jolt went through her. So did the pain, and even though she heard her phone buzzing with a text, there was nothing she could do about that, either.

Rayna had no choice but to fall back into the ditch.

"RAYNA DIDN'T ANSWER," Ian relayed to Court.

Court knew that wasn't good. Especially since Rayna had answered the other texts from Ian. And this one had been important because it had been an order for her to stay put.

Where the heck was she? And why hadn't she answered?

Court grimaced and bit back some profanity. He could feel the blood on his arm. Could feel the pain, too, where the bullet had sliced across it. It wasn't a deep cut, but he would need stitches. Eventually. But for now, he just needed to get to Rayna.

Everything inside Court was yelling for him to get to her. Because he knew something was wrong.

Ian had sent that first text before Court could stop him, and Rayna now knew that he'd been shot. Despite Ian's assurance that it wasn't serious, she probably thought he was dying and would try to help him. That would almost certainly put her in danger, and unlike him, she didn't even have any backup. Heck, he wasn't even sure she knew how to defend herself if it came down to it.

"You know you shouldn't be doing this," Ian warned him when Court climbed out of the ditch.

Yeah, he did, but that wasn't stopping him. Nothing would.

"You should wait here," Court told Ian, but he knew that wasn't going to fly. This was a stupid idea, but Ian wasn't going to let him go out there alone.

Something that Court had allowed to happen to Rayna.

He cursed the fire that had shot up between them. He cursed their attacker, too, for putting them in this situation. Now he only prayed he could get to her in time to stop whatever was happening.

Somehow, Court made it out of the deep ditch onto the pasture grass. And he immediately got slammed with a wave of smoke. He had no choice but to cough, which only made his arm hurt even more. He ignored both the pain and the coughing and started moving. He also kept as low as he could while keeping watch of that treed area where he'd spotted the shooter.

No sign of the person now.

That didn't make Court feel better. Because it could mean their attacker had gotten to Rayna.

That caused him to hurry. Well, hurry as much as he could, anyway. Everything seemed to be working against him, and it didn't help that he didn't know how far she'd managed to go. Hopefully, though, she had stayed in the ditch where he could find her. But even if she was close by, it wouldn't be easy to spot her with the smoke and darkness.

The fire was dying some, but there were still some flames in spots being fanned by the wind. There was still enough of a threat from the shooter, too, that he couldn't give the fire department the green light to enter the area.

But when Thea and John arrived, they would almost certainly get as close as they could. In some ways that would make this situation even more dangerous.

Because Court didn't want the deputies hit with friendly fire. Ditto for the deputies shooting toward Ian and him.

Court and Ian were both on edge and braced for a fight. Not the best conditions for having other lawmen arrive on the scene. Especially since Ian and he were having to keep watch all around them.

Court stopped when he heard a sound. It was like a gasp, and it had come from just ahead of them. He stopped for a second to see if he could pinpoint it. And he did hear something else. A thud. As if someone had fallen.

That got him moving even faster, but Court was well aware he could be walking into an ambush. At least there were some trees to his left that he could maybe dive behind if the shooter was lying in wait for them.

He got a break from a gust of wind that cleared a section of the smoke, and he saw some movement in the ditch. He heard another moan, too.

Hell, it sounded as if Rayna had been hurt.

Nothing could have stopped him at that

point. He readied his gun and ran toward that sound. The wind stopped cooperating though, and the smoke slid right back in front of him, stinging his eyes and blocking his view.

The moment he made it past the fire, Court climbed back down into the ditch. It was clearer there, and he finally saw more than just movement.

He saw Rayna.

She was on her feet, and at first he thought she was okay. Then Court saw someone standing behind her. And that someone had a gun pointed at her head.

Before Court could even react, that someone pulled the trigger.

He watched in horror as Rayna fell, and for several heart-stopping moments he thought she'd been shot.

But she hadn't.

She had dropped down just as the shot had been fired. She was moving, trying to get away, but it was as if she was dazed or something. Her attacker had no trouble latching on to Rayna and dragging her in front of him.

Except it wasn't a *him*.

With the gun back at Rayna's head, the shooter yanked off the gas mask she was wearing, and Court got a good look at her face.

Whitney.

Rayna glanced back at her, too, shock and then anger going through her. But Court got only a split-second glance of both Whitney and Rayna before Whitney turned the gun on him.

And she fired.

RAYNA TRIED TO shout a warning to Court, but her mouth still wasn't working well just yet. That stun gun hit had caused her muscles to spasm, and if Whitney hadn't dragged her to her feet, she'd probably still be on the ground.

On the ground and fighting to save Court.

Thankfully, Court and Ian climbed out of the ditch and scrambled behind some nearby trees, but before they could make it to cover, Whitney shot at them again. Since the gun was right against Rayna's ear, the sound was deafening, and she groaned in pain. She prayed that groan didn't send Court racing toward her though. Because Whitney would almost certainly shoot him.

But why?

Rayna didn't know why a woman she'd once considered her friend would now want Court and her dead. One thing she did know was that Whitney was trapped—something she probably hadn't planned on happening. No. By now, she'd likely thought she would have been able to kill Court and her and then escape.

"Backup's on the way," Court shouted out. "Let Rayna go, and we can talk."

"Talk," Whitney repeated like profanity. "It's a little late for that. Rayna should already be dead, but if I shoot her now, then you'll shoot me."

Rayna hadn't thought for a second that the shot Whitney had aimed at her had been some kind of bluff. No. It was meant to kill her. Except Rayna had managed to fall just in time. She might not get that lucky again.

She wiggled her fingers and toes, trying to get back the feeling in her body so she could fight off Whitney if she tried to pull the trigger again.

"Why are you doing this?" Rayna had to ask. But as soon as the question left her mouth, she thought she had the answer. "Bobby Joe. You're the one who helped him hide all this time."

Whitney didn't jump to deny that. "I was in love with him," she told her "And he threw it all back in my face. He was coming back to town to confess everything."

That didn't make sense. "You mean confess that he'd tried to frame me for his murder?"

"No. To confess that *I* had tried to frame you for his murder."

Oh, mercy.

She couldn't imagine that being true. Until she remembered how Whitney had changed after Bobby Joe's disappearance. And that'd happened because Whitney had fallen in love with him.

"Bobby Joe helped with the framing, at first," Whitney added a moment later, "because he had to collect some of his own blood. But then he had *a change of heart*. That's what the SOB called it. A change of heart, and he was coming here to try to win you back."

Rayna felt the sickening feeling wash over her. "It wouldn't have worked. I would have never gotten back together with Bobby Joe because I've always been in love with Court."

A burst of air left Whitney's mouth. A laugh, but definitely not from humor. "Too bad Bobby Joe didn't know that before he died."

"You mean before you killed him," Rayna snapped.

Whitney didn't deny that, either.

All the missing pieces suddenly fell into place. Well, many of them, anyway. Whitney would have had the chance to get both a spare key to Rayna's house along with the code for her security system. That would have made it easy for Whitney to send a hired thug to break in, drug her and then set her up for Warren's shooting. That same hired thug had probably been the one who'd fired shots at them at the hospital.

The same one maybe who'd taken Court's mother.

Unless the guy was out here somewhere. But Whitney didn't seem to be waiting for her own version of backup. No. Her jerking motions and gusting breath told Rayna that Whitney had been backed into a corner and was now looking for a way out.

"You thought if I was in jail for Warren's murder that Bobby Joe wouldn't try to get back together with me," Rayna concluded.

Still, no denial, and every bit of that silence cut Rayna to the core. She'd been a fool to trust this woman.

"Whitney?" Court called out again. "This is the last warning you'll get. Put down that gun."

Rayna couldn't be sure because she was still light-headed, but she thought maybe Court had moved farther to the right. Whitney must have thought so, too, because the woman shifted their positions, putting her back to the ditch while keeping Rayna in front of her.

"If you try anything, Rayna dies," Whitney shouted back. "Since she just confessed to me that she's in love with you, I doubt you want her dead."

That caused Rayna's chest to tighten even more than it already was. Whitney's outburst wasn't something she wanted Court to hear. Not like that. And not now. He didn't need any more distractions.

"I didn't want my father shot. Or Jennifer and Hallie dead, either," Court responded. "But you killed them. Killed Mitch and Bobby Joe, too. You know what that makes you, Whitney? A serial killer. And people aren't going to go easy on you just because you work for the sheriff's office."

Whitney made a loud sob, and Rayna didn't think it was fake. No, that was real emotion, and Whitney was probably just now realizing the horrible things she'd done. A string of murders that had all started because she wanted to keep Bobby Joe away from Rayna.

There was some more movement, and even though Whitney was crying now, she still pointed the gun in those trees. Which meant she was probably pointing it at Court or Ian. No way was Rayna going to let her claim another life.

Rayna knew she still wasn't steady, but that didn't stop her. She could tell from the way that Whitney tensed her arm that she was about to pull the trigger. That was why Rayna gathered all the strength she could and rammed her elbow into Whitney's stomach.

Whitney howled in pain, cursed.

And she turned the gun on Rayna.

Even in the darkness Rayna could see the hatred in the woman's eyes. Could see that Whitney was going to kill her.

The shot came. Blasting through the air. And Rayna braced herself for the pain. It didn't come though. But there was pain on Whitney's face. Along with some shock. That was when Rayna saw the blood spreading across the front of Whitney's top.

Court stepped out from the trees. He had his gun in his hand, and it was aimed at Whitney.

The woman looked down at the blood, then at Court before she laughed again. Like the other one, there was no humor in it.

But there was *something.* Something evil.

"You might have put a bullet in me," Whitney said, "but you'll never see your mother again. By the time you get to her, she'll be dead."

Whitney dropped to the ground, gasping on the last breath she would ever take.

Chapter Eighteen

Court's mind was shouting for him to do a dozen things at once. He needed to get to his mother, to save her, but he had to make sure Rayna was safe, too. Whitney appeared to be dead.

Appeared.

But since the woman had already murdered at least four people, Court didn't want to take any chances. He scrambled into the ditch so he could get Rayna out of there.

"Your mom," Rayna said. "We have to find her."

Yes, they did, but first they had to confirm that Whitney was indeed dead. Court kicked the woman's gun away from her hand and touched his fingers to her neck to see if he could feel a pulse.

Yes, she was dead all right.

"She hit me with a stun gun," Rayna muttered.

So, that was why she was so wobbly, but it could have been worse. Whitney could have used a real gun, and the only reason she hadn't was because she'd intended to use Rayna as a human shield to try to make an escape. And now even though Whitney was no longer a threat, she still could claim another victim.

His mother.

Ian hurried out from the trees, his gun pointed at Whitney. He didn't get in the ditch with them. He stayed in the pasture keeping watch. He also gave the all clear for backup and the fire department to come closer.

Because they could possibly use it to track the person who'd kidnapped Helen, Court went through Whitney's jeans pockets and located her phone. Actually, there were two of them. One was probably the one she regularly used, and the other was likely a burner cell that couldn't be traced. He put them both in his pockets.

"You're bleeding," Rayna added when he scooped her up and lifted her out of the ditch. Not easily. His arm was still throbbing, but he had to take her to the cruiser so that she wouldn't be out in the open.

The night was suddenly filled with flashing lights from the approaching deputies and the fire engine. With Rayna still in his arms, Court started moving with Ian right behind them.

"You shouldn't be carrying me," Rayna protested. "You've been shot."

That was true, but Rayna wasn't in any shape to run and probably wouldn't be for at least another couple of minutes. Those were minutes he didn't want to risk her being in the pasture.

The moment Court reached Ian's cruiser, he got her in the back seat, and Ian took the wheel. The deputy radioed backup to let them know they were about to drive out of there. Good move, since Court didn't want the other deputies thinking they were perps trying to make an escape.

Despite Rayna still being shaky, that didn't stop her from checking his arm. It was still bleeding, which was probably why she made a slight gasping sound.

"Here's a first-aid kit," Ian said, passing it to her when he took it from the glove compartment. Rayna immediately got to work applying a bandage to Court's arm to slow the bleeding. "Should I take you directly to the hospital—"

"No. To San Antonio. I need to help Egan look for our mother."

Neither Rayna nor Ian argued with him

about that. Probably because they figured it wouldn't do any good.

Because he needed it, Court brushed a quick kiss on Rayna's mouth. She looked up at him, their gazes connecting for just a second before he took out his phone and the two he'd taken from Whitney.

"Glance through those and see who Whitney called," Court told Rayna.

He'd put his own phone on vibrate when he'd gone into cover by the trees and had three missed calls. Two from Rachel and another from Egan. He pressed in Egan's number. And his heart sank when his brother didn't answer. He tried his sister next, and unlike Egan, she answered on the first ring.

"Court," Rachel said on a rise of breath. "Are Rayna and you okay?"

He'd expected her to blurt out some bad news about their mother, so the question was somewhat of a relief. "We're fine. Ian, too." He paused a heartbeat. "Whitney's the one who had Mom kidnapped."

"Whitney?" Rachel repeated, and her tone said it all. She was as shocked as Court and Rayna had been. "Why would she do that, and where does she have her?"

He didn't want to get into the "why," but he

had also been hoping that Rachel would know the "where."

Hell.

"God, Court. Why did Whitney do this?" she repeated.

"To get back at Rayna. Maybe to get back at me, too, for helping Rayna." Or Whitney could have been hoping to set up Helen some way and pin the murders on her. "When's the last time you heard from Egan, because he's not answering his phone?"

"About fifteen minutes ago. He said he was getting ready to meet with the kidnapper."

Now it was Court's turn to be shocked. "Meeting with him? How'd Egan find out where he was?"

"The guy made a ransom call to Egan. It was a man, and he sounded frantic, like maybe things weren't going as planned."

Maybe because he'd realized that the woman who'd hired him was dead or about to be dead.

Rayna held out Whitney's phone for Court to see. "Is that the kidnapper's number?" she asked.

Court read off the number to Rachel. "Yes, that's it," Rachel verified.

Whitney had called the man multiple times in the past two hours. And not just during that time frame, either. When Court scrolled through the history, he saw that Whitney had been calling the man often for the past two days. That was the link they needed to prove that Whitney had hired him. And it was the reason the woman had no doubt used the second phone. It almost certainly wasn't a number assigned to her actual name.

"The kidnapper's using a burner cell so Egan couldn't trace it," Rachel went on, "but the guy wants Egan to meet him and give him some money."

That was good news and bad. Good because the kidnapper would almost certainly keep his mother alive if he wanted to ransom her. But it was bad, too, because it meant Egan could be hurt or killed in an exchange like that.

Court debated if he should call the kidnapper's number, but he decided to wait a few more minutes. Until he'd heard from Egan. If he called now, he might distract his brother at a critical time. It could make things even more dangerous than it already was.

"Please tell me Egan didn't go alone," Court said.

"No. Griff and another Texas Ranger are with him. Egan said I was to wait here, but I'm going crazy. I have to do something to help Mom. I have to do something to stop this."

"You can help her by staying put." Court made sure he sounded like a lawman giving an order and not just like a big brother. "Rayna and I are on the way there to the hospital. I'll drop Rayna off with you and go out and help Egan. Do you know his location?"

"No. He wouldn't tell me."

Probably because Egan hadn't wanted Rachel to try to follow him. But Court could track Egan through his cell phone, since it wasn't a burner.

"Court was shot," Rayna blurted out. "He should see a doctor."

"It can wait," Court said at the same moment Rachel said, "Shot? You said you were fine."

"I will be," Court assured his sister. "Or at least I will be once Mom and Egan are safe." And after he'd made sure that Rayna was okay. Then there'd be time for stitches. "We're about thirty minutes out."

"Forty," Ian corrected.

"Light up the sirens and get us there in thirty," Court told him.

"Stay put," he repeated to Rachel, and he ended the call so he could try Egan again.

Still no answer.

Rayna gave his bandage another adjustment, and when he looked at her, Court saw the tears in her eyes.

"I'm okay, really," he assured her.

She shook her head and blinked back more of those tears. "This is all my fault."

Court had known she was going to say that before the words had even come out of her mouth. Since it wasn't her fault, and he didn't want to hear her continue with an apology, he kissed her.

All in all, it was an effective way to put an end to it. An effective way to make him feel instantly better, too. He was still in pain, but he no longer cared. After several moments, he didn't think Rayna cared, either, because she moved right into the kiss, and she only broke it when she took in a huge gulp of breath.

"You're trying to distract me," she said with her mouth still very close to his. Close enough for him to kiss her again, so that was what he did.

"Yeah," he admitted. "But I need distracting, too." After all, his mother was a hostage, and his brother was out there trying to rescue her. Something that Court wanted to be doing.

Rayna nodded, eased back even more, and he saw the look in her eyes. She was about to apologize again. This time it would no doubt be for his mother.

"None of this was your fault," he said. "Put the blame right on Whitney where it belongs."

She nodded again, but the agreement didn't seem very believable. "I shouldn't have trusted her. I mean, I always knew she had feelings for Bobby Joe, but I thought it was just a crush. I had no idea she was in love with him."

"That seems to be going around," Court muttered.

Her eyes widened. Because she knew they weren't talking about Whitney now. They were talking about her.

"You told Whitney you were in love with me," Court reminded her, though he was certain it wasn't a reminder she needed.

Those words were no doubt as fresh in her mind as they were in his. But it might not be true. The fear and the adrenaline might have caused her to blurt that out.

"Yes," Rayna answered.

She glanced in the front at Ian, but the deputy was on the phone with Thea. Besides, Ian had almost certainly heard what Rayna had said to Whitney.

"It's true. I am in love with you." Rayna's

voice was barely a whisper, but Court still heard it loud and clear.

"You're in love with me?" he said just to make sure. Though he didn't want her to take it back.

She nodded but didn't add more because a ringing sound cut through the silence. It wasn't his phone though but rather one of Whitney's. And it was the kidnapper's number that appeared on the screen.

Court steeled himself as much as he could. Even though he wanted to rip this guy limb from limb, he reined in his temper and hit the answer button.

"Whitney?" someone said. But it wasn't the kidnapper. It was a voice Court recognized.

"It's Court," Court answered. "I have Whitney's phone. She's dead."

"Good. Because I just found out from this piece of slime that Whitney's the one who hired him."

Court hoped that meant Egan had not only the kidnapper but their mother, too. "Is Mom okay?"

"She's shaken up but fine. Not a scratch on her even though she did try to fight off the kidnapper. Griff is taking her back to the hospital right now."

"She's alive," Rayna said, her breath rushing out.

"Yeah," Egan verified. "And it's good to hear that Court and you are, too. What happened?"

Rayna shook her head, obviously not trusting her voice and motioned for Court to give the explanation. He would, but since he didn't want to repeat a lot of the details in front of Rayna, he just kept it simple.

"Whitney killed Jennifer, Hallie, Bobby Joe and Mitch. Then she tried to kill Rayna and me." The woman had almost succeeded, too.

"That's what I got from her hired thug. By the way, his name is Burris Hargrove, and he's talking even after I read him his rights."

"Good." Because Court was sure they would need some details filled in, and Hargrove was the only one who might be able to do that. "How'd you catch him?"

Egan took a deep breath first. "I met Hargrove at the drop site he arranged. It was a gas station about two miles from the hospital. We'd agreed that I would bring thirty grand in cash."

Not much, considering the McCalls were worth millions, but then maybe Hargrove had asked for such a small amount because he'd figured Egan would be able to get it together quickly. Then he could have used it for a fast getaway.

"When I got to the gas station," Egan went on, "I had Griff and Ranger Jameson Beckett come up behind Hargrove. He had Mom gagged and tied up in his car, so Griff got her out of there before Hargrove even knew what was happening. Jameson moved in behind Hargrove so we could trap him. I offered him a choice. He could put down his gun or I'd kill him." There was plenty of anger in Egan's voice. "He put down his gun."

So, Egan had managed to rescue Helen without any shots being taken around her. That was something at least. But he was certain these nightmarish memories would stay with his mother for a long time. They'd certainly stay with him, and he could add nearly losing Rayna to those memories.

"Did Mom say anything?" Court asked.

"Plenty. She was mad Hargrove took her, and she tried to punch him. I let her get off a swing before I pulled her back."

Even though he hated that his mother had

been through that ordeal, this was a normal reaction, and he much preferred it to her breaking down again. Maybe that meant this situation wouldn't interfere with her treatments and healing while she was trying to get her mind back in a good place.

"What about Dad?" Court pressed. "Was it Hargrove who shot him?"

"He says no. He claims the only thing he did was fire shots at Rayna and you, but that he didn't intend to kill you. Yeah," Egan snarled when Court huffed, "I'm not buying that, either. I think Whitney got riled because her plan to set Rayna up wasn't working, and she gave Hargrove the order to kill her. That order probably included you if you got in the way. Which you would have done."

Definitely. No way would Court have just stood by while some snake attacked Rayna.

Rayna's forehead bunched up. "But why did Whitney stop the attack at the hospital?" she asked. "Hargrove had us pinned down. He could have carried through on her orders to kill us."

Court figured he knew the answer to this. "We had backup moving in fast. It wouldn't have been but another few minutes before the deputies would have gotten to him. Whitney wouldn't have wanted us to catch—and interrogate—her hired thug because he might have implicated her."

Rayna made a sound of agreement. "That way Hargrove could regroup and come after us again. Which he did."

Yes, he had. Well, maybe the man had done that. They might never know if it was Whitney or Hargrove who'd fired at them near the sheriff's office. Or set that fire in the alley. And it really didn't matter. Whitney was dead, and whether Hargrove realized it or not, he'd be charged with accessory to murder, which would carry the same penalties as murder itself. The man would probably get the death penalty.

Court was going to make sure that happened.

"The CSIs are still going through Bobby Joe's room at the inn," Egan explained. "But I'll get a team out to Whitney's place, too. I'm betting we'll find some other pieces to this puzzle there."

Probably. And one of those pieces might explain the recording they'd found on Bobby Joe's laptop. Court was betting that Whitney made the recording so that it would look as if Bobby Joe still wanted to go after Rayna.

He hadn't.

Though it did sicken him to think that Bobby Joe had come to town in an attempt to win Rayna back. There'd been no chance of that happening, but Bobby Joe might have turned violent again when Rayna turned him down. No way would Court have allowed the man to get away with something like that.

"I need to get Hargrove to jail," Egan went on a moment later. "Ranger Beckett will help me with that. You're on your way to the hospital now, right, so you can check on Mom?"

"We are. We'll be there in about twenty minutes, maybe less. And before Rayna says anything, I probably need a stitch or two. I got grazed by one of the bullets Whitney shot at us."

"The cut is deep, and he's bleeding," Rayna corrected.

Egan cursed. "Make sure my knot-headed brother sees a doctor as soon as he gets to the hospital."

"Don't worry, I will," she answered right before Egan ended the call.

Since she sounded adamant about doing that, Court figured he wouldn't be able to delay getting those stitches. That meant he needed to finish up whatever he was going to say to

Rayna now, because once they arrived at the hospital, things could get hectic fast.

"I'm glad you told Whitney you were in love with me," he said. "And I'm especially glad you meant it. It saved me from asking you how you felt about me."

She stared at him, obviously waiting for something, and he was pretty sure what that *something* was.

"I've cared about you for a long time," he added and would have said more if she hadn't interrupted him.

"Yes, but that stopped when you thought I got away with murder."

"No, it never stopped." He was certain of that. "So, this isn't exactly love at first sight. It's me finally coming to my senses and admitting something I should have admitted to you ages ago—that I'm in love with you, too."

He'd been so sure she had expected him to say that. Judging from her shocked expression, she hadn't.

"Uh, should I pretend I'm not hearing this?" Ian asked.

"Yes," Rayna and Court answered in unison.

Rayna continued to stare at him, and despite everything they'd just been through, she smiled. Then she kissed him. The kiss was a lot hotter and went on a lot longer than it should have, considering that Ian was only a few feet away from them.

When she pulled back from the kiss, the smile was still on her mouth. "You're in love with me," she said as if that were some kind of miracle.

"Oh, yeah," he assured her.

It wasn't a miracle, either. She was a very easy person to love. Not just for this moment. But forever.

And that was why Court pulled her right back to him for another kiss.

* * * * *

Look for the next book in
USA TODAY *bestselling author*
Delores Fossen's
THE LAWMEN OF McCALL CANYON
miniseries,
FINGER ON THE TRIGGER,
available next month.

And don't miss the books in her
previous series,
BLUE RIVER RANCH:

ALWAYS A LAWMAN
GUNFIRE ON THE RANCH
LAWMAN FROM HER PAST
ROUGHSHOD JUSTICE

Available now from Harlequin Intrigue!

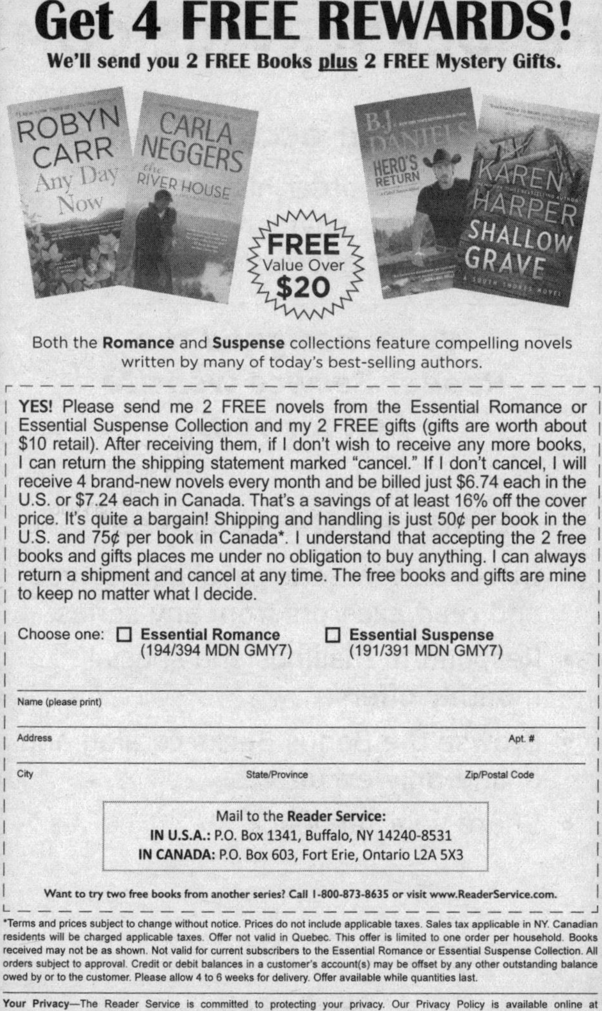
Get 4 FREE REWARDS!
We'll send you 2 FREE Books plus 2 FREE Mystery Gifts.
ROBYN CARR
Any Day Now
CARLA NEGGERS
the RIVER HOUSE
B.J. DANIELS
HERO'S RETURN
KAREN HARPER
SHALLOW GRAVE
FREE
Value Over
$20
Both the Romance and Suspense collections feature compelling novels written by many of today's best-selling authors.
YES! Please send me 2 FREE novels from the Essential Romance or Essential Suspense Collection and my 2 FREE gifts (gifts are worth about $10 retail). After receiving them, if I don't wish to receive any more books, I can return the shipping statement marked "cancel." If I don't cancel, I will receive 4 brand-new novels every month and be billed just $6.74 each in the U.S. or $7.24 each in Canada. That's a savings of at least 16% off the cover price. It's quite a bargain! Shipping and handling is just 50¢ per book in the U.S. and 75¢ per book in Canada*. I understand that accepting the 2 free books and gifts places me under no obligation to buy anything. I can always return a shipment and cancel at any time. The free books and gifts are mine to keep no matter what I decide.
Choose one: ☐ Essential Romance (194/394 MDN GMY7) ☐ Essential Suspense (191/391 MDN GMY7)
Name (please print)
Address
Apt. #
City
State/Province
Zip/Postal Code
Mail to the Reader Service:
IN U.S.A.: P.O. Box 1341, Buffalo, NY 14240-8531
IN CANADA: P.O. Box 603, Fort Erie, Ontario L2A 5X3
Want to try two free books from another series? Call 1-800-873-8635 or visit www.ReaderService.com.
*Terms and prices subject to change without notice. Prices do not include applicable taxes. Sales tax applicable in NY. Canadian residents will be charged applicable taxes. Offer not valid in Quebec. This offer is limited to one order per household. Books received may not be as shown. Not valid for current subscribers to the Essential Romance or Essential Suspense Collection. All orders subject to approval. Credit or debit balances in a customer's account(s) may be offset by any other outstanding balance owed by or to the customer. Please allow 4 to 6 weeks for delivery. Offer available while quantities last.
Your Privacy—The Reader Service is committed to protecting your privacy. Our Privacy Policy is available online at www.ReaderService.com or upon request from the Reader Service. We make a portion of our mailing list available to reputable third parties that offer products we believe may interest you. If you prefer that we not exchange your name with third parties, or if you wish to clarify or modify your communication preferences, please visit us at www.ReaderService.com/consumerschoice or write to us at Reader Service Preference Service, P.O. Box 9062, Buffalo, NY 14240-9062. Include your complete name and address.
STRS18